WARNING

This book contains scenes that some people may find disturbing, including scenes of gory violence. This book is intended for an adult audience and may not be suitable for some people. Reader discretion is advised.

This book is a work of fiction. Any similarities to real places, people or events are purely coincidental.

Cover: @Jertrond
Illustrations: @Pastèk
Editing : Makency Hudson
Copyright © 2023 by Aiden E. Messer.
All rights reserved.

Acknowledgement

Many thanks to @Jertrond for his wonderful work on the cover, Makency Hudson for her great advice and editing work, @Pastèk for their wonderful illustrations, and my parents for agreeing not to read this.

Table of contents

Chapter 1: The Burning Skies 1

Chapter 2: After the World Ended 9

Chapter 3: The New Normal 25

Chapter 4: Pet 41

Chapter 5: Surgery 65

Chapter 6: Welcoming the Darkness 87

Chapter 7: Eye-Catching 107

Chapter 8: The Plan 119

Epilogue: 3 months later 135

Chapter 1: The Burning Skies

The day the world ended started like any other day. In fact, it even started as a significantly good day for Caleb Turner. Caleb was a 22-year-old office clerk with dark skin and kinky light pink hair. That morning, he had won all the FunQuiz games he had played on the subway on his way to work, a little old lady had complimented his hair, and most importantly, his manager had offered him a promotion.

An administrative assistant had recently left the company, and his supervisor thought he would be a good fit. As usual, he had spent his lunch break with his favorite coworker, Nivitha Kumar. Today she was wearing jeans and a dark green t-shirt; a color that Caleb found especially nice on her. Caleb thought she was beautiful with her shiny black hair, curvy body, and nose piercing, but what he found most attractive about her was her imagination and persistence. She never gave up, no matter how difficult the task, and always found creative solutions to problems. In fact, in Caleb's opinion, she should have been the one to get the promotion. She had been working there longer and was among the most efficient employees.

"Yup, but life's not fair, haven't you heard?" she had answered with a bitter laugh when he had told her. "But I don't blame you, it's those managerial bastards' fault. And you deserve it too, let's be honest."

When they returned to the office, the rain that had been falling since the morning had gotten worse, and the wind blew their umbrellas over as soon as they attempted to open them. They ran through the storm, covering their heads with their jackets, and arrived at the office soaked and laughing. Nivitha breathed heavily.

"I haven't run like this since high school," she huffed between two laughs. "And believe me, I didn't miss it at all!"

Caleb gave her a falsely disappointed pout.

"I take it you don't want to run next month's marathon with me?"

Caleb wasn't much more athletic than his friend. His hobbies of choice being macramé and partying, but one of their coworkers had spent several months trying unsuccessfully to convince the entire office to run the marathon with him. A flash of lightning, immediately followed by a loud thunderclap, drowned out Nivitha's answer.

Caleb did his best to focus on his afternoon tasks despite the unrelenting storm. It was getting severe, and he couldn't help but ask himself if it would be dangerous to go out in these conditions. The forecast had only predicted heavy rain, but they were clearly wrong. If the storm didn't calm down, he might not be able to go home. The prospect of having to spend the night at the office didn't thrill him, but at least he would be with Nivitha, that was something. He might work up the courage to invite her to the Ialtag Pub on Friday night, it would be nice to see her after work. He looked at her out of the corner of his eye. She was struggling to hear a customer on the phone over the din of thunder. He gave her a sympathetic smile and headed for the copy machine. He was halfway through his copy when the power went out, plunging the whole building into darkness, lit only by frequent flashes of lightning.

The windows gave off a sanguine glow that caught his attention. He approached, along with several of his coworkers, and his heart sank. A fire tornado moved in their direction, burning everything in its path. Outside, people were running and taking refuge where they could. Many fell, knocked off their feet by debris torn off by the storm, or sometimes struck by lightning, their screams overshadowed by the storm.

Caleb wondered how it was possible that no one in the office had noticed anything, and why no alarm had sounded. In the distance he could see buildings collapsing, devoured by flames. The city was engulfed in panic and chaos, and the office soon joined.

Commotion erupted, causing a frenzy as people panicked and shrieked. He had only one thought in mind: to get out of the building before it collapsed in order to take refuge in the first cellar or underground passage he could find where he would be safe from the fire. Caleb rushed to the stairs alongside with Nivitha, elbowing his way to the exit four floors below. He almost fell several times, pushed by the panicked crowd. Others did fall and Caleb saw people stop to help them up, but he continued on without slowing down, not wanting to be crushed or burned to death. The building had begun to quake, he could feel the heat of the fire tornado and the reverberations of windows shattering around him. He knew he didn't have a minute to spare.

When he reached the outside, his lungs filled with smoke. The crowd cleared, some running to their cars or shelter, some calling for loved ones, others searched for water as a desperate means to assuage the flames.

Caleb ran frantically while scanning his surroundings. Ash and panic filled his throat and lungs, suffocating him. His eyes stung, and his vision was blurry. He felt like he was going to faint any minute, when his gaze fell on a cellar window to his right, partly hidden by a small bush. He kicked it with all his might. Nothing happened. His pink Vans were definitely not fit for the task. Caleb looked around, at the edge of despair, and saw a stone that the storm must have carried there. Throwing it against the small window proved more effective: This time, the glass shattered and Caleb slid inside, ignoring the shards that left long red marks on his body, tearing his shirt and denim jacket, causing some of the badges that covered it to tumble to the ground with small clangs.

He landed in a small cluttered room, filled with shelves loaded with cans, tools, old photo albums, electronics, and toys. Caleb rummaged around in the dark until he found a pack of bottled water and a box full of children's clothes, probably outgrown by their owner. He wet the clothes and used them to block the broken window and prevent the smoke from passing, then drank one of the bottles, hoping to soothe his burning throat and lungs, and poured the rest of the water over his aching eyes.

It was only then that he thought of Nivitha. His heart clenched with shame as he realized that he hadn't thought once about the woman he was supposed to have a crush on, or about anyone else, since he first saw the fire tornado. He grabbed his phone and dialed, his fingers trembling with worry and exhaustion, but he had no signal. Caleb considered going back for his friend, but it was too dangerous and he was too scared, so he curled up in a corner of the room instead, tugging mechanically on his pink leather bracelet that he never took off. He sincerely hoped that Nivitha was okay, as well as his other friends. His thoughts turned to his family. He hadn't spoken to them since he left home at the age of 18, and he didn't regret it. His parents had never made the slightest effort to accept him as he was, and he had no positive feelings towards them. He still remembered the disgust in their eyes when he had come out as bisexual. He still hoped they were okay, but he had no desire to see them ever again.

Nivitha did not immediately understand why her coworkers were screaming and running towards the exit, but when she looked out the window, the horror of the situation exploded before her eyes. She joined the crowd and finally reached the outside. Looking around for Caleb, she saw him crawling into a cellar. She sighed with relief and jumped into her car to rush towards her parents' house. The wind rocked the car dangerously, and she narrowly avoided a tree branch that flew towards her windshield, but she didn't care. She had to see her family, make sure that they were safe.

When she reached the neighborhood where her parents lived, she was horrified to see that it was already on fire. She ignored her body telling her to stay as far away from the oppressive heat as possible. With a heavy heart, she ran to the house. Her sister, Asha, was crying on the porch, cradling their father's body, her long light blue dress stained with ash. She raised her head when she heard Nivitha. Her brown face was also covered in ash, drowning her mole in a sea of gray spots. She stammered:

"He came back for me. He was almost out, he... he should be alive. Not me."

Nivitha fought back her own tears. She would have time to grieve later, but for now she had to protect her baby sister, and find their mother. Of course, at 19, Asha was far from being a child. She was now a beautiful young woman, small and slender, with long coal silky hair, the tips of which were dyed blue and reached the middle of her back. Nivitha knew well that her tendency to overprotect Asha sometimes annoyed her, but Asha was still so young, so naive and innocent. It was probably because she was 6 years older, but Nivitha had always felt responsible for her sister.

"Don't say that, Ashy, that's not true. Just hide in the basement, okay? I'm going to find mom, and I'll come back with her."

The basement was accessed from the outside, and it was the safest place she could think of at the moment.

Asha wiped her eyes with the back of her hand and raised her head.

"No, I'm coming with you."

Nivitha scratched her nose ring nervously. She really didn't want to argue with her sister now.

"Asha, please..."

"I said I'm going with you. You're not mom, and I'm not 10 anymore." her voice softened. "Let's look out for each other, okay? I can't lose you too."

Nivitha felt the tears running down her cheeks. She didn't want to put her sister in danger, but she could see that she wouldn't change her mind, and they couldn't stay like that in the middle of burning houses any longer.

"Fine, but promise me you'll be careful."

"I will. You, too, be careful."

Nivitha burst out coughing uncontrollably, and realized that in her haste to find her family, she hadn't done anything to protect herself from the smoke. She tore the bottom of her t-shirt, ripping through the fabric with great difficulty with the help of her key's sharp ridges. Covering her mouth and nose with the cloth, she urged her sister to do the same, and they set off. The determined sisters decided to make the trek to their mother's work. It wasn't far and the dangers far-outweighed the thought of not seeing their mother again. They weren't sure that it was much safer than driving, but they didn't like the idea of being cooped up inside a vehicle during a firestorm.

Chapter 2: After the World Ended

Caleb awoke in the cellar. He had no idea how much time had passed since the disaster, nor did he remember falling asleep. His throat and eyes were still stinging, and he drank a second bottle of water before he dared remove the clothes and take a look outside. A nauseating smell of overcooked meat assaulted him as he was faced with a vision of horror. The storm had calmed down, and the fire tornado had passed, leaving only a few small flames burning sporadically. There was almost nothing left of the area, except for damaged buildings and burned corpses, all covered with a coat of ashes.

Caleb stumbled backward and fell to the ground, unable to accept what he had just seen. Caleb took deep breaths as he prayed Nivitha was not amongst the dead. His prayers were interrupted by a massive coughing from the smoke permeating the air. Gathering his courage, he climbed out of the window and began to examine the bodies in spite of his repulsion. Some were so small that they could only belong to children. Some were alone, others were huddled together in a desperate gesture of protection. A melted doll was squeezed in a tiny scorched hand.

With each body he examined, Caleb's stomach grew a little more queasy, but he was forced to admit the truth: they were too badly burned for him to recognize any of them. He had just finished circling the building when he noticed that while most of the vehicles had partly melted or been smashed against buildings and trees, Nivitha's car had just disappeared. He checked around to be sure, but found no trace of her blue Ford Focus. Tears of relief streamed down his face. Nivitha had escaped, he was sure, her ingenuity must have been the main component of her escape. He refused to believe it could be otherwise.

Now that he was reassured about his friend's fate, Caleb pondered his next move. His phone still had no signal, he was alone, there was no chance for the subway to still be functioning, and he had no idea how widespread the devastation was.

For lack of a better idea, he decided to walk towards his apartment, which was about 2 or 3 hours away on foot. Hopefully, he would get out of the destroyed area quickly and find help, maybe even explanations. He wandered through the ruins and corpses for a long time. The warm autumn air was permeated with the acrid stench of corpses, and he found it increasingly difficult to keep from vomiting. A smoldering baby carriage stood in his way, and it was suddenly too much. He collapsed and retched everything he had ingested. The vomit burned his already sore throat and filled his mouth with a sour taste. Caleb stood shakily and moved away from the baby carriage, terrified of what he might see inside. He wished he had taken one of the water bottles with him, but he didn't go back for one. He was sure that if he went back into the cellar, he would crumble into a corner and never have the courage to get out again.

Some time later, Caleb came across a haggard-looking woman in her fifties, whose hair would probably have been black if it hadn't been completely covered in ash. She hobbled towards him.

"Does your phone have reception?" she asked in a hoarse voice, "I need to talk to my family."

Caleb checked again, even though deep down he already knew the answer.

"No, sorry. Do you know what happened?"

"No, there was fire, I hid, my family... I need to get to my family!"

Her voice became agitated. She went on her way without another word, and Caleb went on his. The few other survivors he came across did not understand what had happened any more than he did. All looked lost, some were injured, and none were going in the same direction, so Caleb continued on his way alone. He had planned to follow the same route he took by car, but the disaster had made the landscape unrecognizable, and after an hour, Caleb had no idea where he was anymore. He was hungry, thirsty, and his hope of finding a familiar landmark was diminishing by the minute. He cursed himself once again for not taking water from the cellar, and for the first time, he wondered what had happened to the family that owned it. Were they among the charred bodies, stopped in their frantic race for survival by a merciless flame? The little hand clutching the doll, the baby carriage, it could be any of them.

Lost in his thoughts, Caleb didn't notice that he had reached a city that was slightly less devastated than the ones he had passed through so far. The storm had not entirely spared it, but many buildings were still standing. The bodies that lined the streets were less numerous and had been hit or crushed rather than burned. More importantly, many groups of survivors were milling about, looking for resources, loved ones, or answers. Caleb did his best to ignore the crushed and bloody corpses, which seemed more gruesome to him than the burned ones he had seen. Being able to see their faces, their expression, it just seemed so much more real. He made himself look away, took a deep breath, and grabbed his phone, hoping to finally get some signal, to no avail.

One of the groups approached him. The one who seemed to be the leader, a tall East-Asian man who must have been about the same age as Caleb, asked him:

"You just got here, right? Tell us everything you saw, we need all the information we can get. But first, what's your name?"

Caleb studied him. He had medium long black hair, was wearing cargo pants covered in chains, had a large tattoo of a skeletal dragon on his right arm, and his ears and bottom lip were pierced. It wasn't a very reassuring style, but Caleb had learned long ago not to judge people by their appearance. Besides, it would have seemed hypocritical to him, with his pink hair and denim jacket full of buttons and patches. The young man's smile seemed genuine, and Caleb didn't like being alone. In fact, he noticed that no one else in the city seemed to be on their own. Caleb smiled back at him.

"Okay. I'm Caleb."

"I'm Aeron," the East-Asian man answered. "This is Lola," he pointed to a young woman with short strawberry blonde hair decorated by a crown of light blue nylon flowers, matching her eyes. "Here we have Brenna," a light-brown skinned woman with curly black hair and red bangs and a star tattooed under her left eye nodded at him. "Tristan," a restless young man with short brown hair, a blue scarf, looked quickly at him before averting his gaze, "and finally "Isaac."

Isaac, a beautiful young man with red hair, green eyes, and a freckled face, gave him a bright smile.

"Welcome aboard, Caleb! I love your hair!"

Despite the situation, Caleb couldn't help but blush at the compliment from such a good-looking man.

"Thank you, I love yours too. So, how much do you know about what happened?"

"Not much. We were playing video games in Aeron's basement when the storm hit. We stayed there until it calmed down, and when we came out, the city was like this. From what we heard, it's the same for miles. No one has any signal, and the internet seems to be down."

Caleb tugged on his bracelet. Was this the apocalypse? Was the whole world like this?

"We don't know how far it goes," said Lola. "Maybe nearby states or countries are fine and will send help. Maybe not. That's why we have to help each other and learn to survive on our own."

Aeron clapped him on the back.

"Don't look like that, we're gonna make it! With the six of us, we'll be fine."

Caleb nodded. He loved the way they had naturally included him. They were right, they needed to get organized to survive until help arrived. Hoping that help would arrive. He told them everything he'd seen, which wasn't much, and they listened attentively.

Nivitha and Asha found their mother's law office entirely destroyed. Its ruins were still on fire, the metal plate indicating: *Veda Kumar, Attorney At Law*, was lying on the ground partially melted, hardly recognizable, and the sisters knew that exploring the building in search of their mother would sign their death warrant.

"Maybe she got out," Asha suggested in a shaky voice.

Nivitha nodded, and they went to search the surroundings. They found a burned corpse holding a briefcase that didn't look like their mother's. Another one, that had apparently been hit by a piece of debris, was staring vacantly back at them when a moan drew their attention. They rushed towards the noise and Nivitha froze. Their mother was lying on the patch of grass next to the building, breathing weakly. Her abdomen had been punctured by a metal rod, and blood was slowly flowing from her lips. Asha knelt down beside her and took her hand.

"It's okay, mama, it's okay. We'll get you out of here, we'll find a way."

Nivitha was paralyzed. She knew it was too late for their mother, and she felt lost. Veda looked at her, her eyes wet with tears.

"Take care of her..." she breathed before closing her eyes forever.

Asha's heart-wrenching cry brought Nivitha back to reality. She had to protect her little sister at all costs, even more so now that her mother had entrusted her with the responsibility. She gently squeezed Asha's shoulder.

"Come on, we need to find a shelter."

Asha threw herself into her arms. Between two sobs, she managed to articulate:

"I can't... I'm not strong like you, I can't do this anymore."

Nivitha held her close, silent tears streaming down her face.

"We need to survive, Asha. For mom and dad. Please."

Asha took a deep breath and nodded. The worst of the storm seemed to have passed, but Nivitha did not want to take any risks. She moved away from the fires and huddled in a ditch with her sister until the wind died down. They remained mostly silent, and Asha eventually fell asleep in her sister's arms, exhausted from crying.

Nivitha gently woke her up a few hours later, and they wandered aimlessly through the ruined streets, trying not to look at the many corpses. Nivitha soon realized that there were no safe places left here. If she wanted to protect her sister, they had to leave and hope to find a place that was still inhabitable.

"So... Where do we go?" Asha asked as she fiddled with the pin that held her long black hair with dark blue tips.

Nivitha shifted her weight from one leg to the other while looking around. She didn't know what to do either, but she had to make a decision.

"West, to Green Bay. It is a big city, it may have held on better, and the lake may have protected them from the fire."

Nivitha was not at all sure of what she was saying, but she felt better now that she had a goal to hold on to. Asha nodded with a determined look on her face.

"Good idea. It's like a ten-minute drive, we should be there soon."

"With the state of the roads, I don't think that we can take the car. I don't even know if it still works. On foot, it's more like 1 or 2 hours, I guess."

Asha grimaced, but she did not complain, and the sisters set off.

Nivitha and Asha had been walking in silence for almost an hour in a desolate landscape. Nivitha had tried several times to start a conversation with her sister, without success. The young woman seemed lost inside herself. Her eyes were vacant, and Nivitha did not know how to reach her. She understood that it would take time for her to recover from what she had experienced, so she simply walked beside her, thinking about Green Bay. It was the only thing she could do to avoid sinking into despair herself.

Another hour later, Nivitha saw what looked like Green Bay in the distance. Although damaged, the city had indeed withstood the disaster better than what she had seen. From what she could see, most of the damage seemed to have been done by the high winds; the fire tornado appeared to have missed it. Two men who had just left the city approached them.

"Are you from the east? What is it like there, is help coming?" asked the tall bearded man.

"Only a couple hours away," Nivitha answered. "From what we've seen, everything is destroyed. We were hoping to find help here."

The second man, whose black hair was cut short, stared at them with a strange grin.

"Maybe we can help each other. It's not safe for two beautiful young ladies like you to be walking all alone. Be nice to us, and we'll protect you."

Nivitha felt her sister tense up beside her. She quickly scanned her surroundings for a weapon, while answering as calmly as she could:

"Thanks for your offer, but we'll manage. Have a nice day."

The two men stepped closer menacingly, and the bearded one spoke again:

"Come on, don't be shy, it'll be fun. I love chubby brown women like you."

Nivitha repressed a disgusted grimace. She realized that she could not avoid confrontation. Her eyes fell on a sharp branch and she grabbed it, for lack of anything better.

"I said no," she repeated while brandishing the branch in front of her, acutely aware of how ridiculously small it was. "Now leave us alone."

The black-haired man laughed.

"Looks like the tigress got claws. Come on kitten, put that down, you'll hurt yourself."

The bearded man reached out to grab her, but Nivitha was faster. She struck him with her branch, which went deep into his eye. The man recoiled, screaming, and his eye came out of its socket with a sickening *plop*. It had remained on the stick despite being still attached to his face by his optic nerve. A transparent jelly mixed with blood flowed down the branch, which Nivitha dropped in horror. It swung grotesquely against the man's chest, still caught in his eye.

Asha let out a disgusted squeal, and Nivitha froze for a moment. She only meant to make him back up. The second man took advantage of her hesitation and jumped on her, knocking her to the ground. He clasped his hands around her throat, shouting:

"I'll kill you, you fat bitch!"

Nivitha could not push him away. She felt her strength leave her little by little, while panic spread through her. She couldn't die now, leaving her sister in the hands of these monsters. Yet, despite her efforts, the man's hands would not budge. She heard a thud, and the pressure on her neck immediately loosened. Nivitha pushed the man's limp body away and struggled to sit up. The back of his head was covered with blood, and Asha was holding a heavy stone.

Nivitha gently took the stone from her sister's hands and hit the man's head again and again. His skull cracked multiple times and the ground around what had been his face became covered with a red mass of broken bone and crushed brain. She felt powerful and in control.

The other man was still on the ground, holding his bloody eye socket and writhing in pain. His eye and the branch lodged in it, swung at the end of his optic nerve to the rhythm of his tremors. Nivitha smashed the stone against his face, crushing his nose into his skull. She repeated the movement until the stone was covered with blood and brain matter.

Once she was confident that both men were dead and she and Asha were safe, she turned her attention back to her sister.

"Are you okay?"

Asha was breathing heavily, and Nivitha saw that she had been throwing up.

"I'm fine, I... I just can't believe that we killed those men."

Nivitha couldn't believe it either. It was the first time she had taken a life, and she had never imagined that she would ever have to. She could still feel the wood sinking into the man's eye and it made her skin crawl. At the same time, it filled her with a pleasant thrill. She had shown those creeps what she was capable of, and they would never assault anyone again.

"They were going to hurt us, Ashy. We had no choice."

The younger woman nervously played with her hairpin.

"I know, I agree. But still, it's awful."

Pet

The two women arrived in the city less than fifteen minutes later. The encounter with the men brought Asha out of her lethargy. She still didn't talk much, but she was more present, and discussed with her sister what they would need to survive. They found several groups of survivors busy organizing themselves. Some wanted to cooperate, while others seemed more aggressive. Nivitha and Asha decided to keep to themselves as long as they could, there was safety in numbers, but they didn't want to mix with strangers after what they had just experienced. They preferred to be with someone they absolutely trusted, while waiting for the governmental help that would surely arrive soon.

They went to a huge supermarket to get water and food. Nivitha didn't like the idea of stealing, and knew her sister wasn't any more comfortable with it. They reassured themselves that this was an exceptional situation, they were only taking what they really needed, and they could pay for it later, when the situation stabilized.

A familiar voice called her name, and Nivitha saw Caleb running towards her. She dropped the bottle she had grabbed and rushed into his arms.

"Caleb! You're okay!"

Caleb hugged her tightly and laughed.

"I knew you would make it! I knew it!"

When he finally let go, he pointed to a group of young adults who seemed to be waiting for him.

"I met these guys, they're really nice. You should join us!"

Nivitha shifted her weight uneasily from one leg to the other. She didn't want to leave Caleb when she had just been reunited with him, but she didn't feel confident about his new friends. They looked friendly and inviting, but something about them made her uncomfortable. Especially the young brown-haired man with the blue scarf and sullen air. She was probably imagining things, and was on the lookout for the slightest danger. She preferred to stick to her initial plan: stay with her sister while waiting for outside help.

"I'm sorry, I'm sure they're very nice, but I'd rather stay with just Asha."

Caleb looked disappointed, and it broke her heart. She cared deeply for him, but she couldn't ask him to give up his friends for her. She almost changed her mind, but a glance at her sister strengthened her resolve. Caleb would do fine on his own, and she had to take care of Asha.

Pet

Chapter 3: The New Normal

Nivitha's refusal to join them felt like a cold emptiness in Caleb's chest. He could understand that she put her sister before him, but nothing was stopping them both from coming. Maybe he had simply been wrong about their relationship, and she only saw him as a nice coworker, and not as a real friend, let alone a potential boyfriend.

Caleb sighed. At least she was alive, and he had more important things than relationships to think about. The group had settled in Aeron's basement. Caleb and Isaac took inventory of all the food and drink they had, while Lola and Brenna were looking for any other useful things - blankets, tools, etc. As for Aeron and Tristan, they were out looking for any information they could find about the situation. Caleb looked at the girls. They couldn't have been more opposite: Lola was petite and thin, short hair, no makeup, and wore a cute pastel tank top and jeans, while Brenna was a little taller and more muscular. She was wearing a dark red lipstick, black eyeliner and eyeshadow, a black pentagram-neckline shirt, dark red short skirt, fishnets, and a choker. Despite their differences, they seemed extremely close to each other. Caleb smiled and resumed his inventory.

"Without counting the beers, the rum, and the vodka, we have enough drinks to hold about one week if we ration a little," he announced.

"As long as we don't ration the beers, I'm fine with it!" Isaac replied with a broad smile.

Caleb couldn't help but notice how his emerald eyes twinkled hungrily every time he looked at him, and he had to admit that the feeling was mutual. Isaac looked away after staring a little longer than necessary, and told the group:

"For food, we can last two weeks, if not more."

Brenna and Lola exchanged a knowing smile.

"One week is perfect," said Lola, smoothing out her pastel blue tank top. "We'll go get some supplies then. If help hasn't arrived, of course."

Caleb didn't quite see how one week was perfect. Of course, it wasn't bad, but a week went by quickly and he would have preferred to have provisions last longer. Seeing the confident and satisfied expressions on his new friends, he figured that they had probably discussed all this before, and this fitted in with what they had planned. Isaac must have noticed his puzzled expression, because he put his hand around his shoulder and explained:

"The first few days could be dangerous, I have already seen several people fighting and it may not get any better. People are afraid, they don't think. In a week, even if no help arrives, things will have time to settle down, people will have gotten the supplies they think they need, and going out for water will be safer."

Caleb frowned. He didn't want to darken the mood, but the reasoning seemed questionable. Tugging on his bracelet, he finally decided to ask:

"What if it's the other way around? What if people see that no help is coming and decide to hoard all the resources?"

It was Lola who answered him with a serious and calculating air.

"I think we should trust others. Studies have shown that in case of disasters, people are actually much more likely to help each other than we tend to think. And if I'm wrong, the lake is not far away. If we boil the water, we should be able to drink it. For food, it's more complicated, but I guess we can always fish or hunt, and even grow plants in the long run if we find seeds."

Brenna gave Lola an approving look.

"This girl is a genius, believe me, as long as she is with us, we have nothing to worry about."

Lola blushed slightly and ran her hand through her strawberry blonde pixie cut awkwardly, displacing her flowery headgear in the process. She quickly put it back in place.

"In any case, I'm not worried about the food. If you're done with the inventory, come help us go through the mess in this cabinet, I'm sure there's still plenty of useful stuff hidden among the junk. We just found a screwdriver under a dirty sock!"

"We'd just get in the way," Isaac answered. "We'll see if there's anything salvageable up there instead. You coming, Cal?"

Aeron's house had been largely destroyed by the storm, but Isaac and Caleb were still able to retrieve more food as well as blankets, towels, and pillows that would be useful for sleeping.

"Do you know what happened to your family?" Isaac asked, "Sorry if this is a sensitive subject, but since you came alone, I was just wondering... I mean, I'm here if you need to talk, okay?"

"It's okay. I don't know what happened to them, we weren't really close, you know. I'd rather not think about it. What about you?"

"Same. They always saw me as a disappointment, so we didn't talk much. *Isaac Montgomery, you will never get anywhere in life if you don't take school more seriously!* You get the idea. Couldn't understand that I didn't have the same goals in life as them. I guess it doesn't matter anymore. I got along quite well with my cousin, Elias, but he left for Europe some time ago. Hopefully things are better there."

Caleb offered him a comforting smile.

"I'm sure they are, and that Elias is fine."

He was about to head back down and join the others, when Isaac grabbed his arm.

"Wait. I know it's a little forward, we've only known each other for a few hours, but... this could be the end of the world.

We don't know what will happen tomorrow. So, yeah, I think you're really cute, and I really like you."

Caleb felt his heart quicken as a pleasant warmth filled his chest. Nivitha's face flashed in his mind, but he pushed the thought away. Clearly, she didn't want him, and Isaac was right: they had no idea what tomorrow would bring, and needed to make the most of today. He gently placed his hands on Isaac's cheeks and kissed him. Isaac returned his kiss hesitantly, then more hungrily. They were startled by the sound of footsteps and pulled apart. Aeron and Tristan appeared. Aeron's face was unreadable, but Tristan looked terrible. He was staring at his feet, biting his nails.

"What happened?" Caleb asked. "Did you learn anything new?"

Aeron motioned for them to come with him downstairs. He took off his leather jacket and, once the group was together, he explained:

"It's not looking good for outside help. We met people coming from different directions and it's apparently the same or worse. It's been almost 24 hours, and nobody has seen any rescue anywhere. There's still no signal. I think we're on our own."

Caleb felt his heart sink. So, it was true, this was really what his life was going to be like from now on?

Aeron continued in a reassuring tone:

"I know, it's scary. But as long as we stick together, all six of us, I'm sure everything will be fine."

Caleb clung to his words. Aeron sounded confident, and he felt he could trust him and the other members of the group. He had to believe in them, in himself, and in their ability to survive together. That was when he noticed a drop of blood on Tristan's shoe. When asked about it, Aeron's face darkened and he gave Tristan a strange look.

"Not everyone is friendly. It's nothing serious, but it's probably safer not to go out alone, just to be sure."

Caleb noticed that Tristan was shrinking even more into himself, more morose than ever, and he preferred not to press the matter. Whatever had happened, neither of them wanted to talk about it.

Lola quickly summarized their inventory, while Brenna brought Aeron something to eat and drink. Caleb was surprised to see that everyone seemed to be avoiding Tristan. Before he had time to wonder, Isaac took him by the arm and led him to sit on an old sofa with him, while Lola handed out beers to everyone.

"To the end of the world, and to our new life together!"

Nivitha's back was hurting. The hair salon she and Asha had moved into was preserved enough to give them the shelter they needed, but the barber chairs made for poor beds. For breakfast, the two sisters ate a bag of cookies they had picked up at the supermarket the day before. Neither of them felt like eating, but Nivitha made herself swallow and urged her sister to do the same. They didn't know when help would arrive, if ever, and they couldn't let themselves starve.

"I can't get it out of my head," Asha said after eating in silence for a while, staring at her hands.

Nivitha nodded. It all still seemed so unreal to her. Even though she had seen the bodies of her parents, she still found it hard to believe that they were actually dead. She didn't dare think about what could have happened to the rest of her family and friends ; the possibility that they could be dead too was far too painful.

"It feels like a nightmare," she answered. "I keep feeling like I'm going to wake up at any moment, in my bed, in my normal life. But that won't happen."

"I don't want this to be the new normal," Asha whispered, her eyes still glued to her hands. "I can't... I... Those men... I can't do it again."

Nivitha then realized that, while their parents' death had obviously impact, it was the death of the two men that haunted her sister. She herself felt a sick sense of satisfaction when she thought about it, but she should have known that it wouldn't be so easy for her sister. She remembered the time when Asha was nine, she came home from school crying because she had accidentally bumped into a girl on the playground, and the kid had scraped her knee in the fall. It was nothing serious, the girl was not even angry with her and no one had scolded her, but Asha had felt guilty for days. Now that she thought about it, her little sister even hated killing chickens in video games because it made her sad. Of course, having taken part in the murder of a man, even if it was entirely justified and in defense, would impact her deeply.

"You did the right thing yesterday. Without you, I would be dead. I don't want this to be the new normal either, and maybe it isn't. Rescue could arrive at any time. In the meantime, we will be careful, we will avoid going out, and I'm sure everything will be fine."

It was a lie, Nivitha was not sure of anything anymore, but she needed to reassure herself as much as her sister. Asha smiled faintly, her eyes glistening with tears.

"I hope you're right. I'm sorry I'm not strong like you. I don't want to be a burden."

Nivitha held her in her arms.

"Hey, don't say that! You're not a burden, and you'll never be! You're strong too, don't ever believe otherwise. You've always been so kind and helpful, and that's something we really need in a situation like this."

Asha wiped away her tears, and spoke in a slightly shaky voice:

"You're right, we need people willing to help in a situation like this. We can't stay cooped up waiting for a potential rescue team to arrive, we have to get out and help the people who need it, ourselves."

Nivitha fidgeted nervously with the cookie bag. In theory, she agreed with her sister, and she was usually the kind of person who would run into danger without hesitation. Only, she wanted to protect Asha at all costs, and the best way to do that was to stay locked up, away from people. On the other hand, Asha was an adult, as she had pointed out herself the day before. She couldn't stop her from making her own decisions.

"Are you sure..." Nivitha began.

Asha cut her off:

"Yes, Niv, I'm sure. It's the right thing to do. And... I know what we did yesterday was justified, and helping other people won't undo it anyway, but..."

"But you hate that you hurt someone, and you want to do good instead." Nivitha finished.

Asha nodded. She wasn't acting only out of guilt, wanting to help was in her nature, but the incident reinforced this need. Nivitha sighed. She could not refuse her sister that.

After promising each other that they would be careful, the sisters went outside to explore the ruins. They entered a building that had largely collapsed, careful that nothing would crumble on them. Inside, they found crushed corpses, their faces twisted by fear or confusion. A low moan drew their attention, and they discovered a woman in her fifties trapped under the debris. Her legs had been crushed by a piece of ceiling, and she was extremely pale. Asha rushed towards her, followed by Nivitha, and the two women joined forces to free her from the rubble. Her legs, visibly broken in several places, had been lacerated by the concrete, and the remaining skin was an alarming shade of purple. She tried to speak, but pain and dehydration prevented her from doing so. Nivitha and Asha exchanged a glance. Neither of them had the medical skills to help her. Nivitha thought for a moment about shortening her suffering, but she couldn't bring herself to do it. Instead, she motioned to her sister to help her, and they moved the debris together and carried her out of the building as gently as they could.

"It's all right, we'll find a pharmacy and take care of your legs," assured Asha.

The woman nodded weakly. Nivitha gritted her teeth. They would need way more than a pharmacy for this. All they could do was disinfect and bandage the woman's legs; it would not be enough. The one they found was in ruins, but a group of people had taken out everything they could and set up a makeshift medic next to it. A young blonde woman was helping an old man with a bandaged arm drink water, a boy no older than 16 wiped blood from a woman's wound, a middle-aged man was comforting a crying little boy. Dozens of people were busy caring for the wounded. Nivitha and Asha were happy to see that so many people had come together to help. A middle-aged man came to meet them and helped carry the injured woman.

"We'll take care of her, don't worry. I'm Rafael. What's her name?"

"We don't know, we found her in the rubble," Nivitha answered.

"You're searching the rubble?" Rafael asked. "That's great. We have people doing it too, but there are so many, we need all the hands we can get."

"Yes, we want to help however we can. I'm glad to see that we're not the only ones!" Asha said enthusiastically.

Rafael winced as he began to examine the woman's leg.

"I wish everyone thought like that. This kind of situation brings out the true nature of people, both good and bad. Earlier today, I saw a young man threaten another with a knife. I think he hurt him, but I'm not sure, I left before they could see me. I wish I had done something about it, but I'm far too cowardly for that, so I help in my own way."

Nivitha did not answer. She understood that the man was scared, and he had the decency to admit his own cowardice, but the idea of letting someone be potentially killed without reacting, without even trying to find other people to do something about it, bothered her.

The Kumar sisters spent the rest of their day taking the wounded they found to the medic, but Nivitha categorically refused to settle down with them.

"They're probably good people. *Probably*. That's the thing, Ashy, we don't know anything about them, and I don't want to take any chances. We'll help them take care of the wounded during the day, but at night we'll go back to the salon, okay?"

Asha had reluctantly agreed. She knew her sister didn't share her optimism, and although she would have preferred to join the group, she was happy to be able to help.

During their second evening together, Caleb and his new friends decide to play *Never Have I Ever*. Tristan didn't seem thrilled with the idea, but he opened one of the bottles of vodka and handed out a shot glass to everyone. The friends pulled cushions and sat in a circle on the floor, and the game began. In turn, each person had to announce an action preceded by the phrase *Never Have I Ever*, and those who had previously performed the action had to drink. Caleb wondered if it was a good idea to drink again, but after all, it might be the end of the world, so they might as well have fun.

"Never have I ever broken a bone." he said.

Brenna chuckled and took a shot. Lola and Isaac grinned at her knowingly and drank too. Aeron shook his head in a mixture of disapproval and amusement, and swallowed his shot.

"Wow!" Caleb exclaimed. "Sounds like a story I need to hear!"

"I'm not sure you'll like it much," Aeron informed him "but we'll tell you sometime. Come on, Isaac, your turn."

"Never Have I Ever... fallen in love with a redhead."

Everyone burst out laughing and Brenna pushed him jokingly.

"Careful, or your head won't fit through that door!"

"Hey! I never said I was talking about me!"

Once the laughter had subsided, Caleb and Aeron took their shots. Caleb made sure to look Isaac in the eye as he drank his. Brenna's turn came next. She thought a few moments before declaring:

"Never have I been drunk before lunchtime."

Isaac and Tristan drank.

"You should drink too, Bren," Lola teased.

"I wasn't drunk! A little tipsy, maybe, but not drunk."

"Never Have I Ever," Aeron began without giving them time to debate, "gotten a scar."

Lola took a shot and Tristan reluctantly joined her.

"You have to tell this one Lola," Aeron said enthusiastically, "it's impressive!"

"If you really want me to. So, Cal, you're the only one who hasn't heard this story yet. I happen to like learning and discovering new things. So, one day, when I was like 7 or 8, I came across an experiment to make fire bubbles, so of course I decided to try it. It said I needed adult supervision, but I was home alone and didn't want to wait for my parents to come back from work. Of course, I dropped the match and it fell right on my belly, burning a hole in my shirt. It blistered and hurt like hell, and since then I have a small burn mark on my stomach."

"The impressive part," Aeron added, "is that instead of crying like any other kid would have, she tried it again and again until it worked! Can you imagine that 7-year-old girl who just burned herself, but refuses to give up? That's our Lola."

Caleb gave her an admiring look. She was indeed impressive. With such a thirst for knowledge, it was no wonder her friends called her a genius.

Lola toyed with the flowers in her hair.

"Anyway, it's my turn. Never have I ever kissed someone I just met."

Everyone drank, except Lola and Tristan. Caleb and Isaac exchanged a discreet smile full of promise. Everyone turned to Tristan, waiting for him to ask his question. Caleb felt a shift in the mood, suddenly slightly more tense.

"Never have I ever sang karaoke."

Everyone relaxed almost imperceptibly, and Caleb promised himself that he would ask Isaac what had happened when he had the chance. This time too, everyone took a shot.

It was Nivitha and Asha's second day working with the medical team. The Kumar sisters had spent the morning scouring the ruins for the wounded. They had already managed to carry three to the nursing station. They would have continued if Rafael hadn't practically forced them to take a break and share lunch with the rest of the team. The man pointed to a short East-Asian man with a buzzcut, two or three years older than Asha.

"This is Lucas Jiāng. He is a nursing student, or at least he used to be before the disaster. He is one of the few people here who has real knowledge of medicine, and the one who had the idea to create this medic."

Lucas gave them a friendly nod.

"Rafael makes it sound like nothing would have happened without me, but if I hadn't been there, someone else would have had the same idea. Anyway, thank you for your work. If you change your mind, there's always room for you in the apartments, you are part of the team."

"We appreciate it, really," Nivitha answered, "but we prefer to stay together, just the two of us."

Asha gave him an apologetic look.

"It's really nice of you, we'll let you know if we change our minds."

Nivitha knew that the end of the sentence was addressed to her rather than to Lucas. It was true that everyone here had welcomed them with open arms, and she understood her sister's eagerness to join them, but it only took one or two ill-intentioned people in the crowd to make it dangerous. They had to get to know them better. Asha and Lucas were chatting happily, and Nivitha turned to Rafael.

"You said that Lucas *used to be* a nursing student. Does this mean that you think the world as we know it is really gone?"

"Well, we can't be sure, but the news from the travelers is not good, and no rescue seems to be coming. I think it's more reasonable to act as if that's the case, hoping we're wrong, than to rely on help that may never come."

Nivitha nodded, her heart sinking. She agreed with him, but hearing someone else say it out loud made it too real for her taste. At least Asha did not seem to be sinking into despair anymore, that was something.

Chapter 4: Pet

Caleb had been living with Aeron, Isaac, Lola, Brenna, and Tristan for a week now, and there was still no sign of a rescue team. The young man was beginning to really believe that this was a apocalypse, and the rest of the world was in the same situation. Although he was worried about his friends, he had to admit the idea didn't terrify him as much as he thought it would. This new life with his new friends, especially with Isaac, was actually quite pleasant. They spent most of their day talking and laughing, Lola seemed to have a realistic plan for food and water for the long term, even if she refused to give any details at the moment, and Isaac continued to flirt discreetly with him. Caleb would have liked to have more time alone with the freckled young man to take things further, but had no doubt that it would happen one day.

The nights were a bit cold, but the group piled up cushions, towels, and clothes on the floor to use as a mattress and settled under the covers. Each night, a different person slept on the couch, and when it wasn't Isaac or Caleb, they spent the night snuggled together, sharing their warmth. It would almost have been pleasant, if not for the nightmares filled with fire, burning children, and disarticulated bodies that regularly woke him up with a jolt.

Tristan was still as withdrawn and moody as the day they met. He had a curious relationship with the other members of the group, as if he had known them all his life without actually liking them, and it seemed mutual. Intrigued, Caleb eventually questioned Isaac about him. The young man played with his metal pendant, hesitating, then answered uncomfortably:

"It's a little complicated. The five of us have been friends since the beginning of high school, and Tris has always been... quiet and reserved. Since he went away to college to become a doctor, we only see him on vacations and he's become even more distant, it's like he thinks he's better than us."

Caleb hadn't noticed that Aeron had been listening to them, and was startled when he laughed.

"Yeah, that's one way to put it. He acts like he's better than us, but believe me, we know stories about him that he wouldn't want people to hear."

Out of the corner of his eye, Caleb saw Tristan curl up in his chair, biting his nails and looking angry. He felt a pang of pity for him, but at the same time, the young man made him uncomfortable, as if he were hiding something, and that something could be dangerous. Whatever happened between them, he seemed to suffer from it. Caleb wondered if he had really done something wrong, or if the group was just refusing to admit that they had evolved differently, and wanting to stay together just didn't make sense anymore. He tugged at his bracelet uncomfortably.

Aeron didn't even look at Tristan. He announced:

"Well, it's been a week, and we're running out of water, as expected. Lola, Brenna, Tristan, you come to get supplies with me. Isaac, Caleb, you stay there and watch the base. I'd rather not leave our stuff alone."

Caleb immediately forgot all his concerns about Tristan. He would finally be truly alone with Isaac!

Once the other four had left, Caleb put his hand around Isaac's green sweatshirt and smiled.

"How about picking up where we left off?"

Isaac shivered. He gave him a warm, yet hesitant smile.

"We don't know how long it will take them, they could be back soon."

Caleb was going to tell him that they could do it quickly, but then realized that this might be Isaac's first time, at least with a man.

"It's ok, we can just cuddle and kiss if you prefer. Or not do anything at all. I don't want you to feel pressured or anything."

The young man regained his composure. He straddled Caleb and ran his hand through his pale pink hair:

"Kissing sounds perfect. I'm sure we'll have all the time we want to go further later."

"I love you." Caleb said. As the words escaped his lips, he realized that he truly meant them.

Isaac's lips were soft and warm, his kisses were fierce, and the next hour seemed to Caleb to last only a few minutes. The two young men quickly adjusted their clothes and hair when they heard the rest of the group return, and exchanged one last knowing smile.

Lola came in, her arms loaded with bottles of water. She was closely followed by Tristan, who carried a bag that Caleb assumed was full of food, even though they still had enough for a solid week.

Behind them, Brenna was laughing, clinging to Aeron's arm. Once inside the room, Aeron pushed her away and planted himself in front of Caleb. Brenna grimaced, but said nothing. At this distance, the star tattooed under her eye looked almost like a tear.

Aeron stared Caleb up and down with a grin and, without warning, he punched him in the face. Caleb stumbled and fell. He stayed on the ground, staring at the young tattooed man with his mouth half open, too surprised to react. *Had he done something wrong without realizing it? Was it because of his relationship with Isaac? But how could it be? No one was supposed to know.* Aeron leaned over him. A wicked gleam shone in his dark brown eyes, and his pierced lips stretched into a large grin:

"What, you really thought we'd be friends with you, dipshit?"

Brenna laughed:

"Aww, poor baby, so naive!"

Caleb had no idea what was going on, none of it made any sense. They had known each other and laughed together for a week, and he seemed to get along with everyone, except maybe Tristan, with whom he'd never really connected. So, what could Aeron and Brenna be talking about?

"What do you mean? What have I done?"

Aeron reached into the bag Tristan was holding and pulled out a pair of handcuffs. Brenna held Caleb still while Aeron tied his arms behind his back. Caleb didn't even think about struggling, still in shock. This was ridiculous.

"Are you seriously this stupid?" Aeron asked.

Caleb was still lost. A little voice in his head whispered that this was punishment for being selfish and caring only about himself during the disaster, but he refused to listen to it. He looked towards Isaac. The green-eyed man was standing back. His face was neutral, but the way he rubbed his fingers together showed his nervousness. He did not look like he was going to step in. Lola had put the bottles down and was observing the scene with a mean smile.

"Tris!" Aeron called, "Give me the muzzle."

Tristan reached into the bag and pulled out a metal dog muzzle with black leather straps. He handed it to Aeron without a word.

Aeron fastened it to Caleb's face, completely covering his mouth and nose. Two leather straps went from each side, one over the ear and one under, while a fifth went over his head, preventing the muzzle from falling forward.

"I don't understand," Caleb tried again. "Why are you doing this?"

Lola approached him and ruffled his hair.

"Because we can, little bitch. Because we can."

"Okay, that's enough," Aeron said. "Dogs don't ask questions."

"But," Caleb began tentatively." A kick cut off his speech and his breath. Others followed, and he curled up on the ground. He still couldn't understand what was happening to him, and bitter tears began to well up in his eyes.

The kicking stopped, and Aeron spoke again:

"I told you to shut up. Now be a good little pet and stay here quietly. We'll be right back."

Caleb was hurting. He was scared, and he was lost. Not even fifteen minutes earlier he was kissing Isaac, as happy as he could be given the situation. Now he found himself tied up and muzzled by those who had taken him in and were supposed to be his friends. How could this be?

Aeron, Brenna, Lola, and Tristan went out, leaving him alone again with the red-haired young man. A breath of hope came over Caleb. He gave him an imploring look.

"Isaac, quick, untie me before they come back."

Isaac pulled on his handcuffs.

"I can't, they took the key with them!"

Caleb could feel the panic rising inside him.

"Find something, anything! Please!"

Isaac searched the basement and came back with a screwdriver.

"Okay, stand still, I'm going to try something," he said, going behind Caleb's back.

He delicately grabbed his bound hands, and Caleb relaxed ever so slightly. The warm, familiar touch made him feel a little safer. A sharp pain invaded his arm.

"Yup," Isaac laughed. "You can cut skin with a screwdriver. I was wondering if it would work."

Panic took hold of Caleb again, stronger than ever.

"What are you doing?"

Isaac crouched down in front of him.

"Oh, honey," he purred. "Did you really think it was real? That I was going to help you?"

Caleb felt like he was falling off a precipice. Isaac still had those same ravenous eyes he'd had so many times when looking at him. This time Caleb caught something else, something he hadn't seen before, or had refused to see. Something that looked awfully like bloodlust.

Tears began to roll down Caleb's cheeks. He felt betrayed, even more than when Aeron and the others had come after him. Everything that happened between them, the glances, the laughter, the cuddling, the shy declarations and the passionate kisses, he had sincerely believed that Isaac felt the same way he did. Clearly, he had been wrong. Caleb still didn't have a clue what they wanted from him. He thought about Nivitha, and regretted not having left the group to go with her and her sister.

"Did it mean anything to you?"

Caleb wasn't sure why he was focusing on this, he was well aware that it was absurd to hold on to a crush when his life was possibly in danger, but he needed to know. Isaac caressed the parts of his cheeks that were not covered by the muzzle.

"Of course not," he said almost tenderly, "are you really that dense? Come on, now, be quiet. I'd love to have fun with you, but the others won't be happy if I start without them."

Caleb fell silent. What little hope he had left had just been crushed under Isaac's shoe, and he didn't want to hear any more.

The rest of the group came back, carrying what looked like a cage. They placed it in the center of the basement, and Caleb realized it was a dog crate.

"In you go," Aeron said as he pulled him into the cage.

Caleb did not struggle. What was the point, they were five, and he was alone and tied up. None of this made sense, and he felt far too empty and lost to react anyway.

One week earlier

When the storm subsided, Aeron and his crew emerged from his basement to find a ruined city littered with corpses. They were completely cut off from the outside world, with no signal and no way of knowing the extent of the disaster.

"Wow, look at that!" Aeron said. "It will probably take a long time for the rescue to arrive. Let's have a little fun while we wait, shall we? No one will notice a few more mutilated corpses."

Brenna grabbed his hand and laughed.

"Yes! Let's do it! Can you imagine, if this was the fucking apocalypse? We could do whatever we want forever without any consequences!"

Lola frowned.

"This isn't normal. Somebody should have seen a storm like this coming, there should have been weather warnings. I'm not saying it's the apocalypse, but something's definitely wrong. I could be wrong, but I have a feeling that we're not the only place that got hit, and we could be on our own for quite some time."

"Even better!" Isaac exclaimed. "Then we have all the time we want to have fun, right Aeron?"

Aeron grinned viciously. He hoped that Lola was right, he was tired of just beating up people in dark alleys, he wanted to step it up.

"Then let's go hunting!"

Brenna and Isaac cheered, and Tristan shuddered. He was biting his fingernails, looking utterly terrified and helpless.

"Wait!" said Lola. "I thought of something. If it's really like this in the other towns, people will surely move to look for help. People who don't know our reputation. If we come across a poor, lonely traveler, we could offer them our help and then turn on them after a few days, when they trust us. That would be even funnier than going after random people, wouldn't it? Bring back old memories. And that doesn't stop us from hunting too, of course, as long as they don't see us."

Once again, Aeron was impressed with Lola's way of thinking. The five of them had met in their freshman year of high school, and their penchant for weed had led them to spend most of their evenings together smoking in the nearby woods. Little by little, Aeron, Isaac, Brenna, and Lola had noticed that weed was not the only thing they had in common. They also shared a morbid penchant for violence and death, as well as sadistic tendencies. This was not the case for Tristan, who had then become the group' designated target. He had thought he could escape them when he left to study medicine, but Aeron liked to see him freak out in their presence far too much to let him go so easily. He would come after him again whenever Tristan returned to see his family for the vacations.

If Lola's plan worked, they would be able to relive the feeling they had felt the first time they had gone after Tristan. The euphoria that had filled them when they had seen in the young man's eyes how betrayed and humiliated he felt. It was a high that they had been chasing ever since, unsuccessfully.

"You're a genius, Lola," the tattooed young man exclaimed. "Let's go, guys! We're going hunting, and if we find someone who fits, we do what Lola said."

Most of the survivors had formed small groups that wandered among the devastation. Aeron and his group looked for an isolated street where they could find easy prey. They found a middle-aged man, alone and injured, who tried to run away when he saw them. Unfortunately for him, a building had collapsed, turning the street into a dead end, and the group quickly caught up with him. They beat him, as they had done so often during their nightly escapades in dark alleys. Aeron saw that Tristan was standing back, as usual, but this time it looked like he was about to try and escape. He let Brenna, Lola, and Isaac have their fun with the man, and grabbed Tristan by the chin.

"You're not thinking of leaving us, are you?" he asked sarcastically.

Tristan froze, his brown eyes filled with terror.

"No, of course not, you know I would never do that."

Aeron snickered. He knew that very well as he had almost absolute control over everyone in his group. With Tristan, it was easy. He was far too afraid to dare to disobey him, and with good reason. It wasn't much more complicated with Brenna and Isaac. The young woman with the star tattoo clearly had a crush on him, and he knew exactly how to tug at her heartstrings in the right way so that she wouldn't deny him anything. It was almost the same with Isaac. Aeron couldn't decide if the redheaded man had a crush on him too, or if it was just intense admiration. Either way he could use that feeling to manipulate him as he saw fit. It had been harder for him to figure Lola out, but he had come to understand how she worked. She was intelligent, but few people took her seriously; too busy admiring her physical appearance. She was grateful to him for listening to her and taking her ideas into account, but also for offering her a chance to explore her darkest impulses. It was this gratitude that would keep her by his side as long as he continued to recognize her genius.

The funny thing was, apart from Tristan, everyone was convinced that they were acting entirely of their own free will, and would be offended if anyone even suggested that he could be manipulating them. He thanked his natural charisma for that. He knew how to talk to people, how to make them like him or fear him.

Aeron pushed Tristan's head away unceremoniously.

"I hope so for your sake. You know what we're capable of if you annoy us, especially now."

Aeron did not wait for an answer. He motioned for the others to move away from the man who was now on the ground, pulled out his pocket knife, and slit his throat. Blood escaped from the gaping wound and the man gurgled for a moment before losing consciousness. Aeron had left people for dead before after beating them, but this was the first time he had spilled blood like this. A feeling of complete power overcame him, and he promised himself that it wouldn't be the last time. Brenna and Isaac took out their knives and stabbed the still warm corpse, laughing.

Lola observed them with an amused, almost maternal air. Aeron came up to her.

"You don't want to participate?"

"He's already dead," she answered in an unmoved voice. "If he can't suffer anymore, what's the point?"

Aeron shrugged. He rather agreed with her, he should have enjoyed it a bit longer before killing him, but there would be more.

"Fair enough, but this is just the beginning. The hunt is far from over, especially if you're right."

They went back to Aeron's basement to clean themselves and get rid of the man's blood, and discussed what they would do with their prey after betraying them.

"We kill them, obviously!" said Brenna.

"Right away, just like that?" Lola asked, "there are so many funnier things we could do!"

"Let's keep them as a mascot then," Aeron offered, "our own little pet, to torment whenever we feel like it"

Pet

Everyone approved and after discussing some more details, they headed back out. The groups of survivors moved away as they passed, scared by their appearance or more likely by what they had heard about them. Lola saw a young black man with light pink hair that she had never seen before, standing on his own. She pointed him out to the rest of the group.

"He should do just fine. One of us could flirt with him, it would be even more effective."

Aeron patted her on the shoulder.

"Great idea, as usual. Isaac, you take care of it."

The young freckled man frowned in alarm.

"Why me? I'm not queer!"

Aeron grinned, enjoying the way Isaac was defending himself as if he was trying to hide something. To be honest, he didn't give a shit whether he was queer or not, as long as he could manipulate him.

"Maybe not, but he clearly is, I mean, look at him! And Tris isn't as charismatic as you, he'd screw it up."

A little flattery, a calm and confident voice, and that was it. Of course, he could also have done the job himself, but no one would dare to point it out, and he wasn't going to bother when others could do it for him.

Present days

Isaac studied the young man in the cage. He was motionless, his eyes unfocused. He seemed even more lost than Tristan had been the first time they had really turned on him. Isaac took a puff of the joint that Brenna handed him, before passing it to Aeron. In the end, getting Caleb to believe that he had feelings for him had not been as difficult as he had feared.

All Isaac had to do was think about what they would do to him after betraying his trust, and his eyes would glow with a desire that Caleb probably took for lust, maybe even love. It was almost too easy. Despite his initial reluctance, he had to admit that he had a good time. Kissing the young man knowing how he would end up was a truly thrilling experience.

After smoking in silence for a moment, Aeron stood up and opened Caleb's cage. Isaac stretched and leaned back in his seat, his hands behind his neck, ready to enjoy the show.

Aeron pulled Caleb out of the cage, and the young man meekly complied, still too shocked or desperate to react.

"Now that's a good dog," Aeron sneered. "Actually, now that I think about it, pets don't need clothes."

Fear flashed in Caleb's eyes as Aeron pulled out his pocket knife, and his will seemed to snap back. He struggled and tried to escape, but with his hands cuffed behind his back, there was little he could do.

Isaac got up and held Caleb still so Aeron could work comfortably. Aeron thanked him with an approving nod, and began to cut away Caleb's clothes, leaving long red marks on his body in the process.

Caleb groaned and writhed, which made Brenna chuckle. Isaac raised his head and saw that Lola was smiling approvingly at them, while Tristan, sitting on the floor, looked like he wanted to disappear.

"Please... why...?" Caleb asked in a pleading voice.

Aeron threw his fist into Caleb's forehead, which wasn't protected by the muzzle. The blow's force was increased by the handle of the knife he was holding, and Caleb's eyes unfocused for a few seconds.

"How many times do I have to tell you?" Aeron snarled. "A pet obeys and doesn't speak. So shut your fucking mouth."

Caleb groaned but said nothing, much to Isaac's disappointment, as he hoped to see him get hit again. No matter, all in good time. They had planned to start slowly so as not to kill Caleb too quickly, but they still had plenty of things in store for him.

Once Caleb was completely naked save for the muzzle, Aeron locked him back in the cage.

"Lola," Aeron called, "candles, please."

Lola walked towards Tristan's bag, a wicked grin on her face. She took out three long red pyramid candles, which she handed to Aeron along with a lighter.

"Here you go!"

Aeron placed the candles on the cage and lit them one by one. Soon, drops of hot wax began to fall on Caleb's skin, as he whimpered in pain and tried desperately to find a position where he could avoid them. It was of course impossible; Lola had made sure of that when they had chosen the crate in a crumbling pet shop.

At Aeron's request, Tristan heated up some canned chili and the group dined while watching Caleb squirm pitifully.

Caleb had been locked in the dog crate for a full day now, without food or water. His body throbbed and burned where the wax touched him, his joints ached, and his throat felt like it was made of sandpaper. The pink leather bracelet he never took off, his jacket, and the rest of his torn clothes had been thrown carelessly into a corner of the room. The humiliation was terrible to endure, but worst of all was the feeling of powerlessness. He missed the reassuring contact of the thin piece of pink leather against his wrist, replaced by the coldness of the handcuffs.

Caleb's stomach rumbled as he saw Brenna pouring dog food and water into two bowls, causing his kidnappers to laugh.

"Aww, look at that, our little puppy recognizes its yum-yum!" Isaac commented.

Caleb turned red, humiliated, but he didn't dare complain, fearing that Brenna would remove the bowls and let him die of thirst. The dark-skinned young woman with the star tattoo opened the cage and let him out. She undid his cuffs and made him crawl to the bowls.

"Bon appétit!" she said, tucking a lock of red hair behind her ear.

Caleb massaged his sore wrists and tried to untie his muzzle, only to find that it was locked. More laughter arose from the group.

"What are you waiting for?" Brenna teased.

Caleb felt panic wash over him. He didn't want to starve to death, he had to find a way. The dark-skinned young man grabbed the water bowl, threw his head back, and tried to pour the liquid into his mouth. A few heavenly drops reached his lips, but most spilled onto his chin.

"Please," he mumbled in a hoarse voice, "I'll do whatever you want."

More laughter. Aeron walked over to him and grabbed his pink hair, forcing him to look at him.

"I want you to shut the hell up. Pets don't talk if I have to say it again, I'll get mad, and trust me you don't want to see that."

Aeron pushed Caleb back and kicked him in the stomach, knocking the breath out of him, before returning to his seat. He took a big gulp of beer and opened a bag of chips, which he shared with his friends, making sure to show Caleb just how great eating was. Caleb struggled trying to remove his muzzle, and then trying to get some food between the metal bars, but nothing helped. He ended up curling up on himself, convinced that he was going to slowly die of hunger and thirst.

After what felt like an eternity, Isaac knelt before him with a key in his hand.

"Don't worry, you're not going to die yet, but soon you'll wish you had."

The ignoble young man removed Caleb's muzzle and kissed him. Caleb winced, too weak to push him away. Isaac released him and refilled the water bowl, then allowed Caleb to eat. Caleb wolfed down both bowls, ignoring the voice in his mind that begged him to keep what was left of his dignity.

All that mattered was to stay alive. When Isaac put his muzzle back on and locked him back in the cage, Caleb was far from being full, but at least his throat was a little less sore and his wrists were no longer cuffed. He settled into the least uncomfortable position possible given how cramped the dog crate was. No one knew where he was, and no one would come to his aide, so he had to find his own way out. If his captors continued to let him out untied to feed him, and if he obeyed meekly, perhaps they would eventually lower their guard, and he could make a run for it. That was a lot of "*ifs*", but it gave him a little hope.

More than a week after the disaster, the arrival of a rescue team seemed dreadfully unlikely. New travelers arrived every day from all over the country. On their way, those travelers had crossed paths with others from other places, and exchanged information with them. The news wasn't good. Violent storms and fire tornadoes had ravaged the entire country, sparing a few cities like Green Bay, but reducing the majority of them to ashes. The same was true for Canada, and probably for other neighboring countries. An increasing number of people became convinced that the apocalypse had arrived, believing the entire planet was engulfed in the same catastrophic scenario.

Nivitha did not believe in the concept of apocalypse, at least not in the biblical sense of the word, but she had to admit that this looked a lot like the end of the world.

"Can you hand me a needle and some alcohol, please?" asked Asha.

The black and blue haired young woman was leaning over a girl who couldn't have been more than eight. A deep cut crossed her leg, exposing the white of her tibia. She had escaped the fire with her parents, but had been injured while they were looking for a place to shelter. Nivitha gave the items to Asha. Her younger sister had no medical training, but she had quickly learned the basics with the makeshift medic team, and she seemed to be in her element. Asha disinfected the needle and wound with alcohol, causing the girl to scream in pain, tears welling up in her eyes.

"I know it hurts," Asha said in a soft, reassuring voice, "but it's important so you can get better, you understand? I can tell you're a brave girl. Just think of something you love, okay? And don't worry, it will be over soon."

She stitched up the wound while encouraging the child. The girl moaned every time the needle pierced her soft flesh, but she put on a brave face.

"And it's done!" Asha said as she tied the last stitch. "You were very brave, well done."

The girl's parents thanked Asha and Nivitha watched the scene, her eyes filled with pride. Her little sister was right, she was no longer a child, and she seemed to have found her place in this new world. She had donned a pair of jeans and a comfortable sweatshirt from the collection of usable clothes amassed by the survivors. As she glowed with an air of belonging, it seemed as though she had always been a part of this place. Nivitha felt much less comfortable than her in this situation. Going to look for wounded in the ruins was fine with her, but after so many days, there were only corpses. Nursing was too delicate for her, and she was afraid of making things worse by making a wrong move. She was content with helping to transport people, preparing materials, and assisting Asha.

Nivitha often thought about Caleb, and wondered how he was doing. She had seen some of his new friends from afar, but never Caleb himself. More worryingly, she had noticed that each time, the travelers seemed to avoid them and look at them with fear. She tried to convince herself that it was only because of their unusual style, but a bad feeling was creeping up on her.

Pet

Chapter 5: Surgery

Aeron pulled Caleb out of the cage. The young man struggled, panicked. He had quickly realized that nothing good happened when he was dragged out. This time was no exception.

After kicking him a few times for good measure, Aeron pulled out his knife while Brenna and Isaac held him down. He caressed Caleb's torso with the tip of his blade, amused to see it rise and fall so rapidly. He pressed the knife a little harder, leaving a trail of blood and fire on Caleb's skin.

The tall man grunted in pain, and Aeron pressed the blade a little deeper. Caleb closed his eyes and bit his lips. He didn't want to give Aeron and his gang the satisfaction of hearing him whimper, but it was almost impossible to hold back.

The knife left his torso and sank several inches into his thigh, opening a long, deep wound, and Caleb screamed. He immediately cursed himself when he heard his captors' laughter, but the pain was too great to resist. A new deep cut in his arm, then in his side, made his screams grow louder. Aeron plunged the blade under the nail of his right thumb and used it as a lever to pry it loose from the flesh. The unbearable pain cut Caleb's breath. Aeron then pulled on the nail to tear it off completely, then stuck his knife under a second nail and repeated the operation. Caleb felt the bile rise to his throat while his whole body tensed up and cold sweat covered him.

Aeron ripped off a third nail as Caleb squirmed in pain, and let Lola check that he hadn't lost too much blood before putting him back in his cage.

"By the way, remember when we played Never Have I Ever?" Aeron teased as he shut the door, "Never Have I Ever broken a bone? Yeah, it wasn't our bones we were talking about."

The next day, Caleb found himself alone in the basement.

It wasn't the first time some of his captors had gone out, only to come back a few hours later covered in blood, but it was the first time they had left him entirely alone. He took advantage of this moment of respite to test the strength of the lock that kept him trapped in the cage. After several violent kicks he could feel the lock begin to crack, but footsteps prevented him from continuing the operation.

Aeron appeared, followed closely by Isaac and Brenna holding a struggling woman. Tristan was right behind, head down, and Lola, next to him, seemed to be keeping an eye on him.

Caleb felt relieved. As long as they were lashing out at her, they wouldn't lash out at him. He had been locked in that cage for five days already and only came out to be burned, beaten, cut, and fed just enough to keep him alive. Everything hurt, and he was on the verge of breaking down.

He was filled with shame at how selfish this thought was, he should feel bad for the woman, and he did, but he was just so scared and exhausted. Brenna and Isaac threw the woman to the ground, and Lola tied her arms behind her back, then her ankles and knees.

"You remember how they did it in the videos?" asked Aeron.

"Of course," Lola answered. "I just need someone to hold her still. And if I mess up, she has two of them, I can just try again."

Brenna and Isaac held the woman still while Aeron made himself comfortable in a chair. Tristan sat on the floor as usual, hugging his knees, his eyes on the ground. Caleb still wasn't sure he understood his relationship with the rest of the group, but it seemed clear to him now that Isaac and Aeron's explanation was bullshit. He seemed more like a whipping boy or something, which explained his morose, withdrawn look. The others now treated him as if he were their slave: made him cook for them, bring them joints and booze, and clean Caleb's cage so that the whole basement didn't smell like shit.

"It's not like it's a real surgery anyway," Brenna said. "As long as there's blood and screams, I'm fine with it, and I know I can count on you for that!"

Caleb felt his heart clench. Whatever they were planning to do to this poor woman would undoubtedly be sickening. The woman must have come to the same conclusion: her breathing quickened and her struggle and pleas became frantic, which seemed to please Aeron's and his friends a great deal.

Lola blushed slightly and readjusted the blue nylon flowers in her hair

"I'll do my best to make you happy."

Lola took out her knife and ripped the woman's shirt open, uncovering a gray triangle bra, which she also cut. Underneath was a pair of pale, slightly sagging breasts. Lola made an incision about 2 inches long in the right one, revealing a mixture of orange fat and light pink tissue. She put a finger in and slid it under the skin to separate the mammary gland from the epidermis of the breast. The woman cried and writhed in pain.

"Ooohh can I try? Can I try?" Brenna asked excitedly.

Lola took her long finger out from underneath the flap of skin, bringing out a few pieces of orange fat in the process. She wiped her hands on her pastel violet flared skirt, staining it with blood.

"Sure, knock yourself out," she smiled.

Caleb nearly "vomited as Brenna, Isaac, and Aeron rummaged one after another under the woman's skin. The woman did throw up, prompting delighted exclamations of amused disgust from Isaac and Brenna. Caleb wondered if he would have a chance to break the lock, rescue the woman, and escape. Lola resumed her work and Caleb sighed. Of course not, the others would catch him immediately, and he didn't dare imagine what they would do to him.

"I still have to remove the mammary gland from the pectoral muscle, and... that's it!" Lola exclaimed, holding up what looked like a piece of mushy meat.

She dropped it on the floor with a soft *plop*, and searched the empty pocket. A gruesome *crack* sounded, and the woman emitted a high-pitched shriek.

"The ribs are right underneath. Here, if I remember correctly, this thing is a piece of rib cartilage." she said, pulling out a small white cylinder.

"Okay, now I understand your passion for surgery videos," laughed Isaac. "That shit is twisted."

Aeron picked the pale pink tissue from the ground and stared at it with fascination.

"Obviously, if Lola is passionate about something, it is always for a good reason, she is our genius after all." He shoved the mammary gland into the woman's throat, muffling her cries and moans, then turned to the young blue-eyed woman. "Do the belly, now, okay?"

The young woman nodded. Caleb noticed that Brenna had grown glum when Aeron had complimented Lola, but she recovered her good mood when the young man tenderly stroked her red and black hair before returning to his seat.

Lola made an arc-shaped incision in the woman's stomach, going almost from hip to hip, and descending to just above the pubic area. The large gaping wound bled less than Caleb had expected. Under the red liquid, the same pale pink and yellowish-orange mush as before was visible. The woman was sweating profusely and gasping for air, unable to spit out her glandular gag. Lola grabbed the skin and pulled slowly, separating the top layer of skin from what was underneath. She lifted the flap of skin and turned it over on the woman's chest.

"Ladies and Gentlemen," Lola announced, "the abdominal muscle!"

She pressed on the pinkish-white tissue, which stretched in a worrying way, as if about to tear. She pressed a little more, until her fingers broke through the membrane, then grabbed a fistful of tissue and ripped it off, like a magician removing a veil.

"And her insides!"

The vision of the brownish-pink and red entrails intertwined with the yellowish fat renewed Caleb's nausea. The woman was still gagging and sobbing, and Caleb hoped for her sake that she would die soon. Lola pulled the sides of the skin and moved the entrails so that her friends had a good view of what was inside, then she let them take over. Caleb was horrified to see how movable the organs were, and how empty it seemed to be around them, like rummaging through a half-empty suitcase. He wanted to close his eyes, but despite his horror, he was unable to look away. Brenna, Isaac, and Aeron had their hands thrust deep into the woman's abdomen and were tearing out the entrails, like a pack of wild animals, filling the basement with the sickening smell of blood and shit. The woman was jerking and blood was flowing from her mouth, until she stopped moving entirely. Dead.

The three of them continued to tear the body apart for some time until they got bored.

Aeron opened the dog crate and let Caleb out.

"You're hungry, aren't you?" he asked as he took the muzzle off.

Caleb felt his heart quicken as a cold sweat broke out on him. He knew that talking would only make things worse, so he shook his head vigorously and gave Aeron a pleading look. He had been persistently hungry and thirsty for days, but this slaughter had taken away his appetite, and he'd rather be hungry than do what he suspected Aeron was going to ask of him.

"Don't be shy," Aeron purred, "eat. Dogs love fresh meat, right?"

Caleb shook his head again, so Aeron grabbed him by the hair and pressed his face into the still warm stomach. The putrid smell invaded his lungs and this time he couldn't help but vomit. Aeron took his pocket knife and slashed deeply into Caleb's right arm.

"Bad pet. I give you good fresh meat and this is how you thank me?"

A new stab slashed across his cheek, filling it with a burning pain.

"Now eat, you stupid mutt. And your vomit too, I don't want to see a drop of it."

Trembling, Caleb complied. He took a small bite of flesh, which he threw up immediately. Aeron pushed his head into the greenish puddle.

"Clean it, you fucking idiot."

Terrified of being lacerated again, Caleb did his best to obey. The sour taste and overwhelming stench burned his throat and made him feel as if he were choking. It was all he could do not to throw up again. Once he was done licking all the vomit from the floor, Aeron shoved his head into the woman's viscera again. Caleb made himself bite into the entrail, breathing deeply to keep his stomach under control. He could feel his whole body trembling. The flesh was chewy and had a strong metallic taste. He swallowed a chunk, then another. Tears of horror, humiliation and disgust cascaded down his cheeks. He couldn't believe that all this was real. Just a few days earlier, he was getting a promotion, and now he was eating human flesh. It was all too much, it couldn't be happening. It was just a weird nightmare induced by too much partying. He was going to wake up in his bed with a bad headache anytime now, he had to.

He took a third bite, and threw up again. Aeron put his muzzle back on and threw him into the cage crudely.

"I should have known you wouldn't even be able to do something that simple. Too bad, you won't have anything else to eat for the next 24 hours, at least."

Caleb noticed the uncomfortable, pitying look Tristan was giving him. He had definitely misjudged him. If he had taken the time to talk to him, to be concerned about him, maybe he would have understood what was going on, and he wouldn't be in this mess. Or maybe it wouldn't have made any difference, maybe it would have precipitated his downfall.

The next day, the group left Caleb alone again. When he walked out of the basement, Tristan turned and gave him a distressed glance. Caleb felt like he wanted to tell him something, but Brenna grabbed him by the arm and forced him to move on before he could say anything. As soon as he heard the main door close, Caleb started kicking the cage door again. This time, the lock gave way with a satisfying *crack*.

Caleb crawled out and got to his feet with difficulty. Aeron and his crew were forcing him to stay on his hands and knees when he wasn't cramped in the cage, and his joints were stiff and sore. He grabbed the key to his muzzle that had been left on a shelf, and untied the instrument of torment, letting it fall to the ground. He then quickly put on his torn clothes, and headed for the exit. The familiar feeling of the pink leather bracelet against his bruised wrist comforted him. He crossed the ruined kitchen. The main door was between two destroyed sections of wall, too high to climb quickly, especially in his state. He wasn't even sure he could walk much more than sixty feet without collapsing. He reached for the doorknob, when a hand on his shoulder made him jump.

He pressed the handle, but the door was locked. The hand made him turn around, and he found himself facing Aeron. Brenna, Lola, and Isaac came out of their hiding spot, laughing. Tristan followed them, his gaze downcast.

"Did you really think we wouldn't notice your little game with the lock yesterday?" Aeron asked. "We'll make you regret it."

Caleb was aware that he probably wouldn't get another chance to escape. If he could force Aeron to let go, he might have time to climb over one of the collapsed walls and flee. He hit his captor with all his might, but wounded and hungry as he was, he only managed to anger the man. Aeron threw him down the stairs to the basement and signaled for Brenna and Isaac to hold him down.

Aeron placed the muzzle back on him and ripped off his clothes, while Lola approached with thread and a thick needle.

"Here's what we do to bad dogs who don't want to keep their muzzles on," she said, sewing the device onto Caleb's face.

The pain was not unbearable compared to what he had experienced in the last days, but he was no less terrified.

Aeron went through a bag and came back with ring screws and a drill with a hook. Caleb paled, his eyes widening in alarm at the sight. His breathing became erratic as Aeron placed the cold tip of the screw against his left wrist. He struggled desperately, to no avail. The high-pitched sound of the drill filled his ears a fraction of a second before an excruciating pain exploded in his arm, so intense that his vision blurred. The screw easily penetrated his skin, and quickly scraped against his radius, producing a more overwhelming sound. Caleb felt as if it was echoing directly inside his brain, and his entire skeleton seemed to be vibrating. The pressure increased significantly, and the screw slowly sank into his bone. When the shrill sound finally stopped and the pain receded, Caleb's body went limp. He felt the prick of a new screw pressed against his other wrist and immediately tensed again, his lungs filled with panic. The shrill sound resumed, and Caleb screamed and writhed in pain, until he passed out.

He regained consciousness as Aeron went after his ankles. The young man drifted in and out of consciousness, his ears filled with the sickening sound of the screwdriver and of metal against bones. By the time Aeron was done, two ring screws were embedded in Caleb's wrists, two more in his elbows, two in his shoulders, two in his ankles, two in his hips, two above his knees, and two in his lower back. He was shaking and sweating profusely and could hardly breathe, even after the drill had stopped.

"The dog crate may not be enough to keep you still, but this should do the trick," Aeron said as he grabbed some steel carabiners.

He watched Caleb thoughtfully for a moment, then turned him onto his stomach. He used the carabiners and ring screws to tie Caleb's wrists together behind his back, then his ankle, his knees, and finally he added a pair of carabiners to the screws on Caleb's ankles and tied them to those on his hips. Satisfied, he threw the young man back into his cage, as his companions laughed.

This time, Caleb truly couldn't move. Even if the carabiners didn't immobilize him, the pain alone would have been enough. He decided that he would not fight anymore; he never wanted to go through that kind of pain ever again. From now on, he would do everything to make Aeron and his sadistic little friends happy, hoping that they would not hurt him and they would eventually get tired of him and leave him alone. Or kill him. He wasn't sure he cared anymore.

Asha was feeling surprisingly good. Of course, she missed her parents every day, and even more at night. She still had many nightmares, but here she felt useful, she felt like she was making a real difference. If the disaster hadn't happened, she would have started studying education in college after the summer break, but now she thought medicine may have been a better fit. It didn't matter now; she would most likely never have the opportunity to study anything. As long as she could continue to help others, she didn't care. She sat next to Lucas and handed him some crackers. The air of the autumn day was still warm, and he had removed his shirt, revealing two thin horizontal scars under his chest.

"How's little Eva? Did you change her bandage?"

"She's fine," Lucas answered, "it doesn't look infected. You did a good job."

"Thanks, I had a good teacher."

Lucas laughed, as he was the one who taught her the basics of nursing, but his face quickly turned serious again.

"What about your sister? Does she really want you to continue living in that hair salon? There's plenty of room for you in the apartments."

There were now many uninhabited apartments in the city, their owners having died during the storm, stranded in other cities where they worked, or decided to leave in search of help. Some were still in good enough condition to be inhabited, and Lucas and his team had chosen a few to settle in, while others were used to house the injured. They had also moved the nursing station, now an infirmary, inside a building to be protected from the weather and some of the nighttime cold.

Asha ran her fingers through her black and blue hair and sighed.

"She has some trouble trusting people. It makes her feel better when it's just the two of us," Asha glanced at her sister who was organizing equipment a bit further away, "but she's getting to know you guys now, she can see that you're not dangerous. I think I'll be able to convince her to move in with you guys soon."

"That's great," Lucas said, taking her hand, "I would love to spend more time with you."

Asha smiled and squeezed his hand, blushing.

"I would love that, too."

In the evening, Asha settled on her mattress next to Nivitha. The Kumar sisters had adapted the hairdressing salon with camping mats and blankets for comfort.

Asha snuggled up to her sister, just like she did when they shared a bed on vacation as children.

"Niv?" she asked, "What if we moved with them? It would make things easier, and I could help if there's an emergency during the night."

Nivitha stroked her sister's hair.

"An emergency during the night, really?" Nivitha echoed with amusement, "Would this emergency be called Lucas, by any chance?"

Asha was glad that the night prevented her sister from seeing that she was blushing.

"No, not at all! I mean, I do like him a lot and I think he likes me too, but it's not just that! We've known them for nearly two weeks now, it might be time to really join the team, don't you think?"

Nivitha remained silent. Asha wondered if she had fallen asleep, but eventually her voice rose again.

"Let's wait a little longer, okay? We can probably trust them, but I'd rather give it another week, just to be sure."

"Okay," Asha replied enthusiastically.

A week would go by quickly, she could wait. She fell asleep hugging her sister, and for once the nightmares in which she saw her parents die in flames were kept at bay by dreams in which she was saving lives with Lucas. At least for some of the night.

Caleb slept very little that night, and the brief moments of sleep were filled with gruesome nightmares, which were still innocuous compared to the reality in which he would wake to. Naked and alone in the metal cage, he shivered with cold. The pain in his battered bones showed no signs of abating. The slightest movement made him want to scream, which he would have done if he wasn't so terrified of attracting his attackers' attention.

The very position he was in was pulling painfully at the ring screws stuck in his body, and it took every ounce of effort he had to remain still and silent. He felt so helpless and abandoned, it was unbearable. On the other side of the bars, Aeron slept peacefully on the couch, which he had claimed for himself since the gang had shown their true colors. Lola, Brenna, and Isaac were still using the pile of pillows and blankets, but Tristan had been excluded. He slept on the floor, protected from the cold only by his clothes and a bath towel.

When Aeron and his group got up in the early afternoon, they completely ignored Caleb, except for Tristan, who frequently gave him sad, uncomfortable looks. Aeron realized this and grabbed him by the throat.

"Do you feel sorry for him?"

"No," Tristan replied in a hoarse voice, struggling to breathe.

"I don't know what's keeping me from killing you right here and now," Aeron snarled as he tightened his grip on Tristan's neck. When the young man's face turned red, he let go, and Tristan collapsed to the ground. Aeron spat at him.

"Make yourself useful and go roll us a blunt."

Tristan got up, coughing, and complied. Aeron sat on Caleb's cage and casually swung his legs. Every time his feet hit the dog cage, a painful shock spread through Caleb's body, until he could not hold back his screams anymore.

"Looks like our little puppy has something to say," Isaac laughed.

"It must be hungry," said Aeron, grabbing the blunt that Tristan was holding out to him with a trembling hand.

Caleb felt his chest tighten a little more. How would he eat or drink now that the muzzle was sewn to his skin? This question, however vital, had not yet crossed his mind in the midst of all this horror, but now he realized that a slow and painful death awaited him.

"Poor pet," Brenna scoffed, "you think it deserves food?"

"It's in a deplorable state," Lola commented, "I don't know if he deserves anything, but I'm sure he's willing to do anything we ask at this point."

"We'll see," Aeron replied.

He jumped off the cage, making sure to shake it as he went, and pulled Caleb out. He undid the carabiners and reattached them so that the screws on Caleb's wrists were linked to the ones on his shoulders and the screws on his ankles to the one on his upper thighs, forcing him to stand on his elbows and knees.

"So, you want to eat?" Aeron asked. "Speak, and if you're a good boy, Lola will have something for you."

Lola cut grabbed a canned soup and a straw, and waved them in front of Caleb's nose.

"See, we've thought of everything. Come on, speak."

Caleb's stomach rumbled at sight. He tried to think quickly, but his brain, numbed by hunger and pain, would not cooperate. The good news was that they weren't planning to let him starve, but he had no clue what they expected him to say. Begging would be the obvious option, but it had never worked before.

"Please," he tried tentatively.

A kick let him know that this was not the right answer. He fell on his side, the pain making his vision go blank for a split second. Brenna put him back on all fours.

"Bad dog," Aeron said. "Now, speak."

Realization dawned on him. It suddenly seemed so obvious that he had to stifle a mirthless laugh. Locking what little dignity he had left in the depths of his mind, Caleb began to bark.

"Good boy!" Aeron scoffed as he petted his pink hair.

"You're right, Lolly," Brenna said, throwing her arm around Lola's shoulder, "he is so desperate he'll do anything."

"I told you I hate that nickname," Lola protested, blushing at Brenna's touch.

She reluctantly pulled herself out of Brenna's arms, opened the soup and added the straw before holding it out to Caleb. The young man struggled to get the straw between the bars of the muzzle, but eventually managed to do so and drank, eyes downcast, while Aeron's gang chuckled and petted him, calling him a good boy.

"Good," Aeron said once Caleb had finished the soup. "Now if you want to drink, walk around the basement."

Walking on his elbows and knees on the hard concrete floor was humiliating and painful, each step reverberating violently in his battered bones, but he clenched his teeth and bore it. He had to be careful to place his knees and elbows correctly so as not to press on the screws. It was hard, but he could handle it, but strongly doubted that he would fare as well with whatever his captors had planned if he didn't comply. Lola was right, as much as he hated to admit it, he was desperate and willing to do anything to reduce his suffering.

By the time he was done, he was sweating profusely, and the agony completely absorbed his thoughts. He collapsed at Aeron's feet, and gulped down the water that Lola handed him. He was so exhausted that he could barely hear the others laughing and making fun of him.

Tristan was doing his best to keep a neutral face. He didn't really know Caleb, but it was obvious to him that he was a good person, and seeing him like this broke his heart. To see anyone in that state would have saddened him deeply, and the kindness he perceived in Caleb - as well as his handsomeness, - only reinforced that. He wished he could hold him, nurse his wounds, and tell him everything would be okay, but doing so would condemn them both. Despite what Aeron had said earlier, Tristan knew perfectly well why he hadn't killed him yet. He loved feeling powerful, and the power he knew he had over Tristan was too satisfying for him to give it up. This would not last forever. If Tristan displeased him too much, he would eventually get bored, and getting killed would be the easy way out. Before the disaster, Aeron and his cronies were always careful not to leave any visible marks when they tormented him, but there was no reason for them to be discreet now. He could easily find himself in the same position as Caleb.

Tristan contemplated the idea of killing himself to avoid ending up like that. He had already thought about running away, but he knew that his former friends were keeping an eye on him. Even if he managed to leave without them noticing, he was too afraid of what Aeron would do to him if he was found. He wondered if his parents were looking for him right now. Probably not. If they had survived the disaster, they most likely hadn't thought of him once. It's not like they were ever really interested in him. There's no way they never noticed something was wrong with him, that he wasn't doing well, but as long as he was getting good grades, they never bothered to check. The only reason he still went to see them during vacations was because his parents wanted to play "happy family", and his presence was their condition to continue paying for his studies. Look where that got him.

Caleb whimpered in pain as Aeron pulled the ring screwed in his shoulders to guide him back into the dog crate. Tristan clenched his fists. He had to do something. He *wanted* to do something. If he could somehow find a way to bring some comfort to Caleb. He'd never dared stand up for himself after what Aeron had done to him, but maybe he could do it for someone else.

So, he decided to stay alive. He was sick of his life being ruled by fear and shame. He didn't know how, but he would find a way to help Caleb.

Isaac's voice brought him out of his thoughts.

"Hey, nerd! Bring us some beer."

Tristan jumped and stifled a gasp, then rushed to open the bottles.

"By the way, we didn't get a chance to tell you," Lola said, "When I went scouting with Isaac last night, we finally saw people trying to farm. Between the ashes and the decaying corpses, the soil should be fertile. When there's nothing left in the supermarkets, we should be able to easily steal their crops."

The mention of a decaying corpse reminded Tristan of the woman they tortured to death. He had carried her foul-smelling eviscerated body away from their shelter with Brenna, and almost retched. He was no longer so sure that he would be able to keep his good intentions.

Pet

Chapter 6: Welcoming the Darkness

Nivitha was disinfecting a scalpel when Asha and Lucas barged into the room, carrying a barely conscious man covered in blood. Chunks of flesh seemed to have been torn off, his right arm was missing, and one of his femurs was largely visible. Nivitha dropped the scalpel, which fell on the table with a metallic clatter, and brought her hands to her mouth, horrified. The sight of blood had never frightened her, and she was used to seeing injured people being brought into the infirmary, but never in such a gruesome state.

"What happened to him?" she asked as she helped them place the man on the operating table that had been set up in the room.

"We don't know." Asha answered, making a tourniquet on what was left of the man's arm. "People found him near the city limits. We think it's a wild animal attack. A cougar or a wolf, maybe."

Like the humans, most of the animals had died in the disaster, but this wasn't the first time Nivitha had heard of one of them attacking a human. A mangled corpse had been found in the city some time earlier with bite marks on it. Upon reflection it was not surprising: if most of their prey were dead, it seemed logical that they would go after humans. Nivitha shivered and hoped that these would remain isolated cases.

Lucas was doing his best to stop the bleeding with Asha's help, but the man had already lost too much blood, and the nursing student didn't have enough equipment or experience. The wounded man's groans became whimpers, and then silence filled the room. Lucas checked his vitals and shook his head.

"He's dead."

Asha let out a small, muffled sob and Nivitha squeezed her shoulder.

"You did everything you could."

"Your sister is right," Lucas said, taking her hand. "We can't save everyone, but we try, and that matters."

"I know," Asha sighed, resting her head on his shoulder, "but I don't think I'll ever get used to it."

Nivitha left the room as Lucas held Asha in his arms. Her sister was in good hands, and she needed some fresh air. She walked towards the field that other survivors had started to work on.

The streets she passed were still in bad shape, but the corpses that littered them when she and Asha first arrived had been buried outside the city, and the wounded taken care of. Step by step, people organized themselves to survive together. Once again, Nivitha thought of Caleb. She had no idea where he might be, and she missed him. She wished she had at least asked where he'd be staying. When she reached the field, she approached an old woman with sunburned skin. She was resting under a tree after clearly having worked hard by the look of her sweaty forehead.

"How are things going?"

"Quite good," the old woman replied with a friendly smile. "We were able to collect enough seeds to feed the whole city once grown. You work in the infirmary, right?"

"Yes," Nivitha confirmed, "but I'm not in the medical team. I help them prepare everything, that's all."

"It is important too," replied the woman in a serious tone. "I saw you when I came a few days ago for my medicine. You are doing a great job, all of you. I'm glad to see that we still know how to help each other."

A man Nivitha had not seen approaching joined the conversation.

"Bernadette's farming knowledge is very valuable to us," he said, placing a friendly hand on the old lady's shoulder, "but I'm afraid she's being too optimistic. We still don't know if everything will grow properly, and last night we saw two strange young people walking around the fields. Bernadette thinks they were just taking a walk, but I'm not so sure. A mean-looking redheaded kid and a girl with some kind of weird flower crown. To me, that doesn't bode well."

Nivitha felt her heart clench. That description sounded a lot like two of Caleb's new friends. Bernadette jokingly slapped his hand and chuckled.

"I have to be optimistic when I'm stuck with a pessimist like you. You make it sound like they're going to come to us in the night and, what? Slit our throats? Eat our unplanted seeds? They are kids, they were probably looking for a quiet place to make out. Feeling threatened because you saw a girl walking around with a flower crown, you are unbelievable."

Nivitha relaxed. The old lady was right, there was nothing to worry about. Caleb was probably out there somewhere, adjusting to this world in his own way with his friends, and she would eventually bump into him again. A hint of worry lingered in the back of her mind, but she ignored it. There was no point in worrying about something she had no control over.

Caleb watched hazily as Brenna set up a ceiling hook under Lola's supervision. He was too exhausted, hungry, and in pain to try and understand their goal. He just knew it was bad, for him or someone else, and he didn't want to find out, but Aeron gave him no choice.

Once the girls had finished with the setting up, he grabbed him by the hair, dragged him out of the cage, and under the hook.

Caleb groaned helplessly as the young man with the piercings attached the screws embedded in his shoulders, lower back, hips, and ankles to the chains that now hung from the ceiling. He realized it was a pulley system when Isaac pulled on a chain with a laugh, lifting him off the ground. Pain and helplessness brought tears to his eyes. He felt as if all his bones were breaking.

He couldn't take it anymore, he had tried to run away, to obey meekly, but nothing seemed to help ease the hell he was in. He had absolutely no control, and what drove him out of his mind, perhaps even more than the pain itself, was the overwhelming sense of helplessness.

Isaac secured the chain and took Caleb's face in his hands.

"Do you still love me?" he asked mockingly.

Caleb did not answer. What difference would it make anyway? He felt so stupid for falling into his trap. Isaac grabbed the muzzle that was still sewn to Caleb's face and pulled on it, drawing him closer. A few drops of blood dripped from the stitches. Isaac planted a kiss on Caleb's forehead and let him go, causing him to sway on the chains. The pain was so intolerable that he had to struggle to stay conscious.

"I told you it would hold." Lola stated, a hint of pride in her voice.

"Well done!" Aeron complimented her. He turned to Tristan. "Give me the whip."

Caleb groaned as he saw Tristan pick up a cat o' nine tail whip, its nine knotted cords swinging threateningly, and hand it to Aeron with his usual dark look. The bite of the first blow

Pet

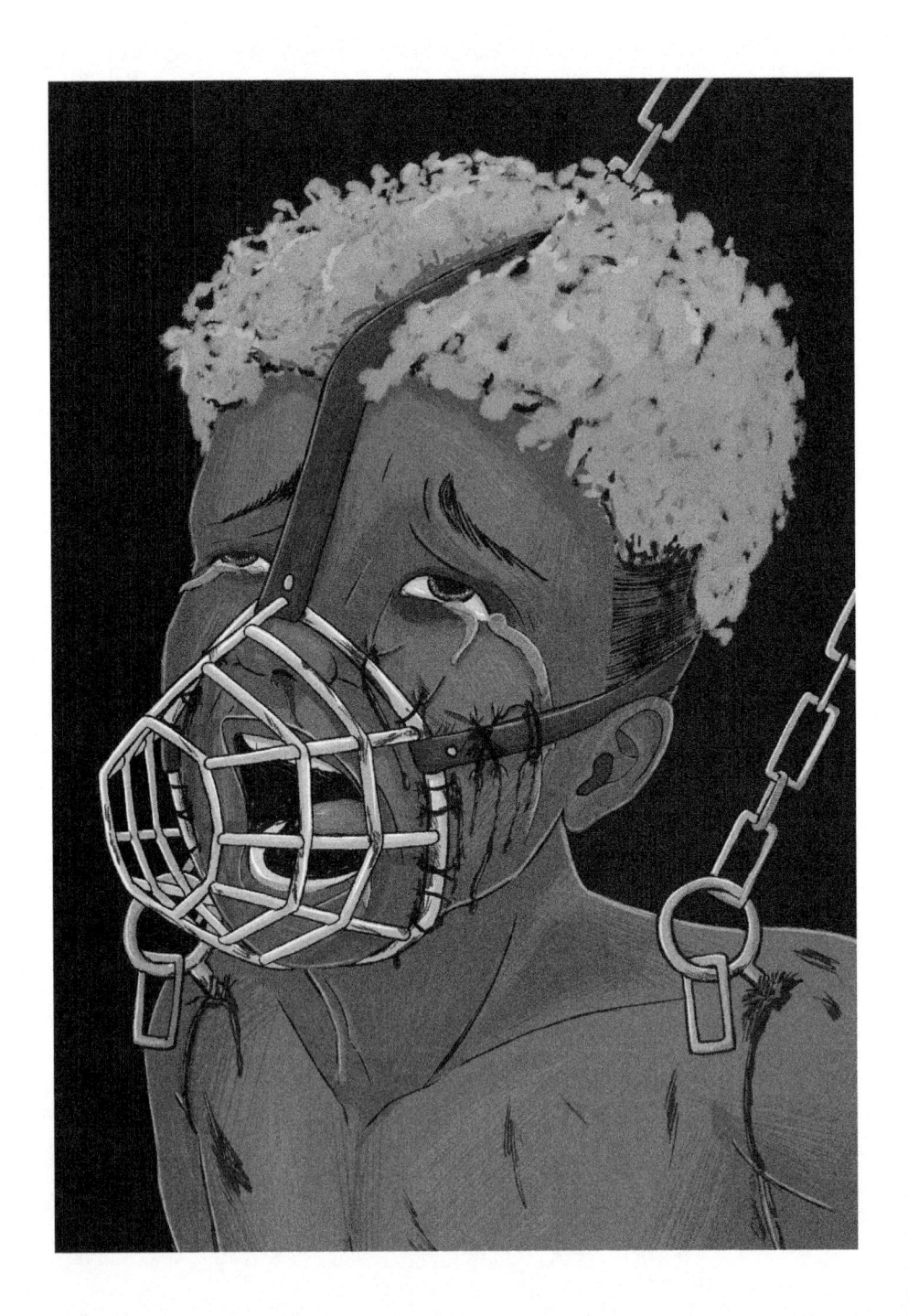

made him jerk, but the pain that this involuntary movement inflicted on his bones was much more intense than the lashes. He unsuccessfully tried to remain as still as possible when the second blow drew a set of burning lines on his flank. A third blow landed on his buttocks, and Caleb wondered why he was battling against unconsciousness. It was his ally; his only possible escape was to take refuge in its arms. He closed his eyes and welcomed the darkness with open arms, but a blow on his back jolted him back to reality. He let out a sob, which was met with laughter from his assailants. Now that he welcomed the nothingness, it was the nothingness that refused him. His last hope of having any form of control, no matter how trivial, had just been ruthlessly ripped away. It was so unjust that Caleb could have screamed if his throat wasn't so dry and sore.

The blows continued to rain down as unconsciousness toyed with him, promising to cradle him tenderly then dropping him mercilessly to return him to pain.

Caleb had no idea how much time had passed when Isaac unfastened the chain and let him fall to the ground. The impact of the concrete floor against his shattered body reverberated in his bones, and darkness finally enveloped him.

Brenna had never been so happy. She felt free and powerful, and could spend most of her time by Aeron's side. Of course, she would have preferred that he pay more attention to her, but he had always been distant. Despite their fooling around and many nights together, he had always refused to make their relationship official. He promised her that even if he had fun with other girls, they didn't mean anything compared to her, and Brenna believed him. She would have done anything for him, and if sharing him was the only way to keep him, then so be it.

As if reading her mind, Aeron put his arm around her waist and pulled her close. She rested her head on his shoulder and strolled through the city, amused to see people move aside and whisper as they passed. They were right to be afraid. Lola, who was walking a few steps behind them with Isaac and Tristan, came up to them. Something seemed to be bothering her.

"We may have gone a little too far," she announced, frowning.

Brenna stared at her in disbelief. Practically everything they had done had been her idea, she couldn't believe that she would let them down all of a sudden. Beside her, Aeron tensed up. He stopped and looked Lola straight in the eyes.

"Here I thought you were too clever to concern yourself with morality. I'm disappointed in you," he said coldly.

Lola looked confused, then her light blue eyes widened.

"Oh! No. No, no, no! That's not what I meant!" she exclaimed before returning to her usual calculating tone. "So far, it's been fun to torture our little pet because he's been reacting, trying to figure out what's going on, struggling, or trying to please us hoping we'll be more gentle with him. But you saw that he hardly reacted when we suspended him. It has a name, it's learned helplessness. He is convinced that no matter what he does, it won't change anything. He's right, of course, but it makes the process much less interesting. Anyway, what I'm trying to say is that if we continue like this, it will soon be like torturing an empty shell. So, in my opinion we have two choices: either we continue and kill him when he becomes too boring, which should happen soon, or we slow down and give him the illusion that he can survive so we can play with him a bit longer. I can't guarantee that it will work if he's already too far gone. What do you think?"

Brenna sighed with relief. Lola was one of her best friends, and she would have been devastated to see her change.

Aeron relaxed and nodded thoughtfully.

"That's an interesting point. I guess we can try to give him back some hope and see what happens. If it doesn't work, we kill him and get a new plaything. It's not like it's hard to find."

The group set out again in search of a new victim to take back to the basement and kill. Brenna thought about the torture session they had indulged in on Caleb a little earlier. He had cried and whimpered, but it was as if he didn't see them. She still had a good time, but it was true that it had been a little disappointing. Lola was probably right, their toy would soon be broken, and they would have to find another one. She didn't mind in the least; it would be fun to find a new pet and see how it would behave and how long it would last.

The sun was beginning to set when the group found a man alone in an alley. Brenna estimated that he must be between thirty and forty years old, not very tall, thin, salt and pepper hair with an unkempt beard. Surely one of those fools who worked in the field and believed in mutual aid, judging by the direction he came from. Brenna smiled broadly. They were going to show him what the real world was like.

Lola leaned against a wall in the basement beside Aeron while Brenna and Isaac tied up the man they had just captured. With five of them, they had no trouble immobilizing him, knocking him out and dragging him back to their lair. Lola glanced disdainfully at Tristan, who was cowering in a corner. As usual, he had pretended to participate for fear of reprisal, without actually doing anything. No one was fooled, but as long as he wasn't in their way, no one cared. Lola wondered if he would ever have the guts to leave. She strongly doubted it; he didn't even dare to look them in the eyes. It was a pity as it could lead to a fun manhunt.

Caleb, still unconscious in his cage, whimpered pathetically in his sleep. Lola winced. This whole learned helplessness shit was really bothering her. She didn't care if they had to move on to a new victim. Aeron was right, there was no shortage of that, but she didn't like that it happened without her planning it. Before the disaster, she spent countless hours reading and researching such topics. She should have thought about it, she probably could have even played on it.

Lola sighed and went over to the man Isaac and Brenna had finished preparing. What was done was done; there was no point in dwelling on it.

"Are you ready for a new surgery demonstration?" she asked with a cruel smile.

Aeron, Isaac, and Brenna cheered, Tristan cowered a little more, and the man, who had awakened, cried out in panic.

Ignoring his boring and unoriginal pleas, Lola turned him over on his stomach, cut off his shirt, and got to work. She made an incision from the back of the neck to the lower back, carefully following his spine. As she had done with the woman some time before, she slipped her fingers between the skin and the flesh and pulled, revealing a garland of vertebrae protruding slightly from the red mush.

The man screamed in agony and pissed himself. Lola sighed. It was a completely predictable reaction, but she would have preferred him to refrain from it. It really lacked class. She changed her mind when she heard Brenna's crystalline laugh, which made the star tattooed under her eye quiver slightly. It was one of her favorite sights, and while it was far from uncommon, it was well worth a little lack of class. Either way, it would be Tristan's job to clean up.

She returned her attention to the open back. The exposed flesh reminded her of pork chops ready for a barbecue, which made her hungry. It probably wasn't that different, she thought. She took her knife and carved out the flesh around the spine to make it more visible.

"Brenna," she called, "can you give me a hand?"

Lola knew that the young woman with red bangs was more muscular than her, and she would be happy to participate.

"I would like you to chop off the spinous process and the laminae on any vertebra. You can even do several of them if you want." she handed her the saw, pointing to a small bony piece protruding from the spine.

"Gladly," the young woman replied while getting down to work.

Hacking through the bone was not an easy task, but Brenna clearly enjoyed it a lot. The man did not. He was twitching and his breathing was labored.

A few minutes later, she handed the three small pieces of bone to Lola.

"Here you go, Dr. Lolly."

Lola rolled her eyes at the nickname, and grabbed the bones.

"I could make them into a necklace for you if you want." she offered.

Brenna's eyes lit up.

"That would be awesome! What do you think, Aeron, would it look good on me?"

Lola did her best to hide her annoyance as Aeron agreed with an uninterested look. She liked him a lot, but Brenna deserved better than this. Lola realized that this scene had cut off her interest in continuing the surgery. She was, however, still hungry.

"The doctor is done for the day," she announced. "If a butcher is willing to come forward, I suggest chops for dinner."

This proposal was met with incredulous and excited exclamations.

"You really are twisted, Lola," Aeron commented with a devilish grin. "So, who wants to be a butcher?"

Isaac stepped forward and skinned the man, who was still groaning feebly. The process was long and tedious, especially since Isaac had no idea what he was doing. He started by grabbing the flaps of skin that Lola had peeled off and pulled until the man's flanks were also raw. He plunged the knife into the flesh and set about carving. Lola sat on an armchair and watched him, trying to divert her attention from Brenna, who was flirting with Aeron. She wasn't sure exactly when the man died, but it had been a while since he had stopped kicking when Isaac finally pulled out something that looked like a bloody, badly cut pork chop. They made Tristan cook it on their gas stove and started to eat. While the taste closely resembled pork in appearance, the texture reminded Lola more of beef.

Tristan looked down at his plate in disgust, a fact that was not lost on Aeron.

"Eat up!" he growled as he shoved Tristan's head into his food.

Tristan was on the verge of tears.

"I can't," he stammered. "I'm sorry, I can't."

Lola was impressed to see him stand up like that. He must have been really disgusted to override his fear. Aeron forced him to his feet and slammed him against a wall.

"You can't? Really?" he asked in a much too sweet voice as he placed his switchblade on the young man's throat. He slowly slid the blade down his torso until it was pressed between his legs. "You know what I can do to you, don't you? So, are you going to eat, or are you going to force me to be mean?"

Tristan's breathing was so ragged that Lola wondered if he was about to have a panic attack.

"I'll eat," he eventually answered with a blank look.

Tristan made himself finish his portion despite the urge to vomit, and barely managed to hold it in. "*You know what I can do to you, don't you?*" Yes, he knew that all too well. He remembered that day during his sophomore year in high school as if it were yesterday, though it had happened five years earlier. The five of them had met at their usual smoking spot in the forest. Aeron had arrived with a struggling stray cat in his arms, and had suggested killing it. Everyone had loved the idea, except Tristan, who had firmly refused. He knew his friends had a thing for violence, but he couldn't believe they would actually do something like that. Aeron didn't appreciate his reaction at all. He had shoved him to the ground and proceeded to kick him. Isaac, Brenna, and Lola had soon joined him. At the time, he had been too surprised to react. The only thing that had come to his mind was that at least the cat had gotten away.

"If you tell anyone about this, I will tell your parents that you are smoking with us," Aeron had threatened.

When his mother had asked him where his bruises came from, Tristan had made up a story about older kids who had stolen his money. He doubted she believed it, but she didn't ask any more questions. She hadn't even tried to find the imaginary thief. It wasn't so much Aeron's threat as the shame that had driven him to lie. His parents had told him several times that he shouldn't hang out with them, they were trouble, and he always refused to listen. He felt bad enough as it was, he didn't want his parents to look at him with annoyed pity and say "*I told you so*".

It was still shame, almost more than fear, that had kept him silent all these years. At first, he had thought it would be an isolated event. His friends had acted as if nothing had happened, and he had tried to do the same and forget. That is, until Aeron pulled out a switchblade a few weeks later while they were out smoking.

Thin white scars now marked the top of Tristan's inner thighs where the blade had tasted his flesh when Brenna and Lola held him down. A body part that Aeron knew no one would see by accident. He could still smell the damp ground and feel the coldness of the leaves and dirt against his cheek, where his face was pressed against the forest floor.

Tristan closed his eyes. He didn't want to think about that. Instead, he took out what was left of the man's body under Isaac's supervision. Once outside, he could not hold himself back and finally threw up, which earned him a blow in the rib and a disdainful remark from Isaac. He cleaned up the blood and piss that stained the basement floor. Caleb was still whimpering in the cage, and Tristan couldn't tell if he was conscious or not. He was beautiful, even in this state. Or rather, his beauty could still be guessed under the dirt, blood and swollen bruises. He should have told him to run when there was still time, but it was too late, and Tristan hated himself for that. Once again, he imagined himself taking him out of this hell and nursing him gently back to health, the way he wished someone would come and save him. It wouldn't cancel out the fact that he hadn't acted when he could have still avoided all of this, and he didn't expect Caleb to forgive him, but at least it would still be better than doing nothing.

When night came, Tristan waited until he was sure everyone was sound asleep before quietly getting up. He had promised himself that he would help Caleb, and he would. Of course, he couldn't free him. Aeron slept with the cage key in his pocket, and even if Tristan had been able to take it, he wouldn't be able to take Caleb very far in his condition. Not far enough to avoid retaliation. Instead, he took a bottle of water and a straw. No one would notice, they had long since stopped rationing them. Tristan lightly brushed Caleb's hand through the bars. The young man flinched and gave him a wary look.

"It's okay," Tristan whispered, "I brought you water."

Caleb stared at the bottle as if it was going to jump out at him at any moment. Tristan's heart clenched. He wanted him to understand that he was on his side, but after all that had happened, Caleb had no reason to trust him. It was no wonder he was expecting a trap.

"I'm so sorry," he finally said, low enough not to wake the others. His eyes were brimming with tears, "I should have warned you, but I was so scared."

Caleb did not answer, but he accepted the water. He gulped down long sips, consistently looking around fearfully. Tristan sat at his side for a long time. Neither of them spoke, but Tristan felt some kind of mutual understanding had passed between them. Or maybe he was just imagining things. Either way, this first act of rebellion had given him some courage, and he was determined not to stop there.

Caleb's throat was aching a little less since Tristan had allowed him to drink his fill. He couldn't decide if he trusted him yet. He had no doubt that he was being bullied by Aeron and his friends, and that he was only staying out of fear, but precisely, they could have been manipulating him. Maybe they had asked Tristan to help him so he could believe he was going to be okay, before taking away all hope again. He did seem sincere, and if it was a trap, he could have warned him somehow. Caleb was far too exhausted to think about it logically. He wanted to believe him, and if it was a trap, he knew he would suffer no matter what he did.

Once again, he regretted not having spoken to Tristan earlier. If he hadn't been so focused on Isaac, he would have been able to see that the young man was suffering, and they may have been able to help each other. When Tristan had apologized for not warning him, Caleb's first instinct had been to resent him. After all, it was true, none of this would have happened if he had said something. Then the woman who had been tortured to death came to his mind. Maybe he could have helped her, but he hadn't done anything either, he hadn't even tried. Just like he hadn't done anything to help anyone during the disaster. If he was honest with himself, he probably wouldn't even have believed Tristan, which wouldn't have stopped the others from punishing him for talking.

Caleb felt a pang of gratitude for the young man. If he had really acted of his own free will, he had taken a huge risk. Considering what Aeron and his gang were capable of, he didn't want to imagine what they would do to Tristan if he found out, or what they had done to him in the past. He wished he could crawl into his arms, feel a little human warmth, and forget where he was, at least for a few moments.

He missed Nivitha so much.

Pet

Chapter 7: Eye-Catching

The sun was already setting when Nivitha and Asha finished their work day in the infirmary. Since Nivitha knew that her period was about to start, she grabbed some pads that were available on a shelf and changed quickly before leaving. The sisters decided to bring Bernadette her medicine to save her a round trip, and to check on the fields. The old woman welcomed them warmly and invited them to share a meal with her and George, the man who had been worried about the two people hanging around the field.

Apparently, no one had seen them again and the work was going well. One of the workers hadn't shown up for a couple of days, which worried George, but Bernadette was sure he had just decided to take some well-deserved time off, or was busy elsewhere and had not thought to warn them.

The old woman was eager to explain to them what kind of seeds could be planted in autumn to be harvested in winter, and they had spent the evening chatting and laughing, so much so that they had not noticed the time passing. This cheerful moment had put Nivitha in a good mood.

"You know what?" she said to Asha on the way back to their hair salon, "You're right. This will be our last night in the salon. Tomorrow we'll move to one of the team apartments. Preferably, the one where Lucas is."

She jostled her sister playfully as she said that last sentence.

"Hey!" Asha protested, pushing her away with a laugh. Her face became serious again, and she added, "Thank you. Really."

Asha was again wearing a long dress, and the light wind made it undulate gently around her, giving her a fairy-like appearance. They were walking through a deserted alley when five people appeared in front of them. Nivitha immediately recognized Caleb's friends. She was about to ask them where he was when the red-haired man and the blue-eyed woman jumped on her. Before she had time to fully realize what was going on, a knife was pressed against her throat. The woman with the star tattoo was holding Asha in a similar position. The tattooed man was watching the scene with a smirk on his face, occasionally glancing menacingly at the brown-haired man who was cowering in on himself.

After a few seconds of silence that seemed like an eternity to Nivitha, he spoke:

"You're the ones we saw with dear Caleb in the store, right? I'm Aeron, and these are my friends Brenna, Lola, Isaac, and Tristan."

"Where is he?" Nivitha asked. "What do you want?"

Aeron's grin grew wider.

"What do we want? But to have fun, of course!" He pretended to think, then spoke to his crew. "Let's kill the younger one. Then we'll take the bigger one home."

Nivitha felt a burning rage rise within her as she struggled against her attackers. These fuckers deserved to die painfully; she would make them regret messing with her. The blade sank slightly into her throat, releasing a few drops of blood, and she stopped, coming back to her senses. She had to keep her little sister safe at all costs, and she would not get anywhere like that, she had to think to find a solution. She quickly scanned her surroundings. There was a piece of concrete torn off by the storm a few steps away from them.

If she could get them to back up enough to trip over it, she might be able to do something. She leaned against them, pretending to try to keep her throat away from the knife, but they didn't move and she couldn't push much harder without it becoming suspicious. Asha was silently crying. The young brown-haired man was biting his nails restlessly. There was no one else in sight, but maybe someone could hear her. She called for help with all her heart, but Aeron silenced her with a punch.

"Keep screaming and I'll slit your throat right now."

Nivitha refused to let panic overtake her and continued to think as fast as she could, but Aeron didn't give her time to find a solution. She watched helplessly as he plunged his knife into her sister's stomach.

Asha looked at her in despair, a dark spot stretching on her beautiful pale dress.

"I don't want to die... Nivitha, please, I don't want to die!" she sobbed.

Nivitha was frozen in shock and fear. *"Take care of her..."* Her mother's last words echoed in her mind as Aeron stabbed Asha once again. Blood was running down her baby sister's lips, and there was nothing Nivitha could do. She felt like she was trapped in a nightmare from which she would never wake. Aeron slashed Asha's belly open, and her innards splattered to the ground with a soft sound. Brenna released the young woman, who fell to her knees and grabbed her organs, trying to put them back in their place with a bewildered expression, but they kept slipping through her fingers. Silently, she collapsed and stopped moving entirely. It took several seconds for Nivitha to realize that she was dead.

Everything seemed so blurry, a moment ago she was laughing with Asha, Bernadette, and George, and now her sister was dead, her guts still in her hands. Confusion gave way to a renewed rage. She would make them pay. She didn't know how yet, but she would find a way, she always did. The group set off and Isaac and Lola dragged her toward their lair. Nivitha looked for any opportunity to escape them, and she got it when Tristan stumbled, dragging Isaac down with him. Nivitha took advantage of this sudden slackening to elbow Lola, who lost her grip on her. She started to run.

Behind her, she could hear grunts of frustration and angry shouts as Tristan knocked Isaac down again while trying to get up. The ensuing commotion gave her the head start she needed to get to the infirmary and lock herself in. The medical team immediately surrounded her.

"Are you okay?"

"What happened?"

"Are you hurt?"

Voices, more or less familiar, echoed around her, but she was unable to focus on them, until Lucas asked her:

"Nivitha? Where's Asha?"

The woman broke down in tears. Between two sobs, she explained as best she could what had happened. She was well aware that her explanation was confusing, but given the dismayed silence that now reigned in the room, and Lucas's horrified paleness, the main point had been made.

"We must find them and avenge her," she concluded.

Tristan held back a sigh of relief when the woman escaped. He put on an apologetic and terrified look - which was not at all difficult, he really did fear for his life - and apologized:

"I am so sorry! I tripped, I didn't mean to cause any trouble!"

That was a lie, of course. He couldn't stand to see them go on their horror spree any longer, and had decided that he wouldn't let them torture Caleb's friend to death in front of him. He knew it would cost him, but if he could convince them that it was an accident, he might survive. If not, he would most likely regret his choice, but at least he saved a life and helped Caleb. Aeron stared at him with an intrigued look on his face. His voice was calm, more curious than angry, which made Tristan shiver.

"Did you really? One could almost believe that you let her get away on purpose."

Tristan felt his breathing quicken and looked down.

"I wouldn't dare."

"True, you're far too much of a pussy for that. But still..." Aeron turned to the others. "What do you think?"

"If he had the balls to do something, he would have done it much sooner," Lola said thoughtfully, "But still, he should get harshly punished to make sure it doesn't happen again, even by accident."

"I agree," Isaac added, "But he still has to be usable afterwards, I don't want to do the cleaning for him."

"Same," Brenna approved.

Aeron made a satisfied face.

"That seems about right. Back to the basement. And Tris, if you try anything funny on the way, I'll kill you."

Tristan was shaking with fear, his heart beating so fast it was painful, the phantom smell of the damp forest floor invading his nostrils. He wondered if being killed would be a better choice, but he knew that with Aeron, it wouldn't be quick, so he just kept walking, trying not to think about what was about to happen. When he entered the basement, he felt like only a fraction of a second had passed, as if the walk back had not existed, like time had warped to make him jump directly to his ordeal.

"Lie down on your back," Aeron commanded.

Tristan complied. His chest was hurting, his mind was dizzy, and he felt like he was going to pass out from sheer terror. The dog crate caught his eye. Inside, Caleb looked at him with an expression he couldn't quite make out beneath the swollen bruises. Compassion, perhaps. Or perplexity. Aeron shifted Tristan until the back of his head was pressed against the crate. He grabbed his wrists and tied them at the top of the cage, then did the same with his neck at the base of the bars. Aeron straddled Tristan and brought his face close to his. Tristan could feel the bile rising from his guts. He squeezed his eyes shut and turned his head away. Aeron grasped him by the chin, forcing him to face him.

"Oh, no, you don't. I need you to look me in the eyes."

Aeron then pushed his thumb into the side of Tristan's right eye. The young man's vision became blurred and stars began to dance in front of him as the finger slowly crept between the eyeball and the eye socket. Despite the intense pain pulsating in his skull, Tristan stood still. If he struggled, he knew he might not only make things worse for himself by pissing off Aeron, but also hurt Caleb by rattling the cage. It became increasingly difficult as the thumb sank deeper into his face, and he couldn't stop several jerks that made Caleb groan in pain, inaudibly under his own screaming. The eye eventually popped out of its socket with a revolting *plop*. Aeron pulled on it and the optical nerve gave way.

"Here," Aeron teased, "I think one eye will be enough for you to do the cleaning, and the other one will remind you what it costs to make me angry."

A dull pain continued to throb in Tristan's head. At least the scars that the blade had left on his upper thigh all those years ago were hidden. Now, every time he would see his reflection, every time someone would look in his direction, he would be reminded of the group and all they had done to him.

Aeron pressed the eyeball against Tristan's lips.

"Now eat it."

Tristan was covered in sweat and felt like he had been drained of all energy. Despite his revulsion, he couldn't think of any way to escape. He opened his mouth and made himself bite. The gelatinous ball exploded in his mouth, releasing a meaty tasting liquid. A harder part crunched under his teeth, and his medical classes came back to his mind: It was probably the cornea. He would have laughed if the situation wasn't so dire; recognizing anatomical parts by eating them, his professors would be proud. The optic nerve and its rubbery texture gave him more trouble, but he eventually succeeded in swallowing the whole thing, to the delight of his tormentors.

Aeron patted his cheek, and this simple contact sent a new wave of pain through Tristan's skull.

"See, it wasn't that hard. Now let's make sure it doesn't get infected. Brenna? Vodka, please."

Grinning broadly, the young woman brought him a bottle. Tristan instinctively clenched the bars in his fists and regretted it instantly when Caleb moaned in pain. He doubted that vodka would really disinfect anything, the alcohol was not concentrated enough. He knew that it would, however, be extremely painful, which was probably Aeron's intention. Something brushed against his hair, and he realized it was Caleb's hand. He didn't know if it was a deliberate gesture or a coincidence, but the touch comforted him slightly. He took a deep breath, and waited. The liquid burned his empty eye socket, and Tristan felt like his lungs were being torn apart by his own screams, but he remained focused and barely rattled the cage.

Caleb wondered what Tristan could have done to receive such treatment. Perhaps they had found out about the water. He wished he could say something to him, to show him that he was grateful and sorry that he was suffering such a fate, but that would only cause them both more trouble. So, he had simply caressed his hair lightly despite the pain that this gesture caused him, in a discreet movement that he hoped Tristan would perceive as friendly. Aeron had untied him shortly after pouring the vodka where his right eye had been, and since then the young man had been sitting in a corner, hugging his knees as he shivered, his greenish face turned towards the ground.

"What about him?" Isaac asked, indicating Caleb with his chin, "We've been leaving him alone for a couple of days, he'll get used to it if we're not careful."

Caleb felt his blood run cold. *Not again. He would lose his mind.* He closed his eyes and tried to calm down. Tristan had helped him despite the risks. He had remained calm while he was being tortured, clearly so as not to rock the cage. Caleb may not be able to thank him directly, but he could hold on to life and to his mind so that Tristan's efforts would not be wasted. When Aeron pulled him out of the dog crate, Caleb didn't struggle. Instead, he held his head high and tried to erase the fear from his eyes.

"Well!" Aeron commented, apparently pleased, "Looks like our dear pet has some fight left in him!"

Caleb almost gave up. What was the point, if every effort he made only amused them more? He met Tristan's gaze and saw in it a timid flicker of hope that strengthened his resolve.

It didn't matter what his captors thought. He wasn't doing it for them, he was doing it for himself, and for Tristan, who had given him some much-needed comfort.

Aeron secured the screws in Caleb's wrists to the ones in his lower back with a carabiner. He repeated the operation by fastening his ankles and then his knees together, then laid him on his stomach. Caleb hated feeling so exposed and powerless, but he refused to let it show. He stared straight ahead with determination, teeth clenched, ready to endure what would come next. Or, more realistically, ready to try and make it look like it wasn't affecting him.

Aeron grabbed Caleb's muzzle and shook it.

"We'll wipe that look off your face quickly, you'll see."

He lit his lighter and the flame danced in front of Caleb's face, licking the muzzle. Aeron reached behind Caleb's back and held the flame against the screw in his right ankle. Nothing happened for several moments, then the metal became warm, then hot, then burning. Caleb felt the flesh around the screw blister and sizzle. It was painful, but so was his every move. He managed to keep a neutral face, even as Aeron pressed the flame directly against his skin, covering his legs, then his back and arms with blisters. Caleb remembered his first night in the dog crate with the candle dropping burning wax on him. The pain had seemed much more intense at that moment. Now it was just another drop in an ocean of agony. Aeron finally put him back in the cage after untying him and made sure to pull on the screws in the process.

"Fine, I didn't make you scream today, but it's only a matter of time," he said.

Caleb noticed that when Aeron and Lola made eye contact, Lola nodded discreetly. Although still shaking, Tristan looked relieved. Caleb didn't know what that could mean, but he realized there was probably a reason Aeron had let him off the hook so easily.

Chapter 8: The Plan

Nivitha was alone in her cold bed in the empty apartment. She had retrieved her sister's body with the nursing team and buried it, but no one, not even Lucas, had agreed to avenge her. They said it was too dangerous, that they didn't know where her murderers were hiding, that it wasn't what she would have wanted. Nivitha sneered bitterly. No, it probably wasn't what her kind, sweet little sister would have wanted, but she was dead now, and revenge was what she herself wanted.

Caleb would never have joined such people willingly, she was sure. This meant that they must have tricked him, and that he must still be in their clutches. She refused to believe that he could be dead. She had told this to Lucas and the others, she had even begged them, if they would not avenge Asha, to at least help her friend. They looked at her with pity, expressing their apologies but explaining their inability to help, insisting that she had to move on. She wanted to slap them, to scream at them until they understood her rage.

Nivitha could not bear to stay with these people who were pretending to mourn her sister without doing anything to stop the people who had murdered her. She couldn't bear to stay in the hair salon she had shared with Asha and that kept reminding her of her absence either. So, she had moved into one of the many abandoned apartments of the crumbling city.

It was strange to live there without knowing if its previous owners were dead or stuck on the other side of the country. Nivitha piled all the photos and personal effects she had found and hid them in various cupboards. It was easier to be in an empty apartment with no personality, that way she could almost forget that it had been the home of someone who may no longer be. She made sure not to throw anything away or damage anything, just in case this person ever came back.

Nivitha had spent the day looking for the gang, without much success. Several people had recognized the description, and she even suspected that some had an idea of where they lived, but no one would give her any useful information. She couldn't figure out if they were afraid for her or of them, maybe a little of both. Either way, everyone was advising her to forget about it and stay as far away from them as possible. Of course, she had no intention of listening to them. She had nothing left to lose except Caleb, and she would undoubtedly lose him too if she didn't do something soon. After she insisted perhaps a little too forcefully, a woman in her thirties had finally agreed to tell her about them:

"Aeron and his gang have always been a bunch of thugs, the kind that beat someone up and left them for dead in a dark alley. I think his girlfriend, the one with the star tattoo, did a few months in jail for drugs, and people said she was covering for him. What I'm saying is, they've always been dangerous, and I'm afraid that's even more true since the disaster. The friend of one of the people I work with at the orphanage knows someone who apparently found a mutilated corpse somewhere. And by mutilated, I mean that one of her breasts had been ripped off, and she had been eviscerated! I'm sure it's them. But this stays between us, I'm not even supposed to know. The people who found her didn't want to cause a panic, and I promised not to tell anyone."

The woman refused to tell her more, and Nivitha eventually went home. She didn't know if this mutilated corpse stuff was true, but considering what they had done to her poor sister, it seemed quite possible. She couldn't imagine what they might be doing to Caleb right now. She didn't like the idea of keeping this kind of information secret, even if it was to avoid a panic. People had a right to know what was going on, but even if she told everyone, she doubted it would change anything. People wouldn't believe her, or tell her to drop it and stay away from Aeron and the others, just like they were doing now.

She went to bed with a sinking feeling in her stomach and the beginning of a plan. She would keep looking for them as visibly and loudly as possible. Eventually it would get back to them, and they would be the ones to find her. This time, she would let them lead her to their lair, and when they least expected it, she would retrieve a knife up her sleeve and rescue her friend. Granted, it still needed improvement, but at least it was a start.

Tristan waited once again until everyone was sound asleep before getting up. He glanced at Caleb, who was shivering in his sleep, but this time he didn't go near the cage. Instead, ignoring his fear, he went upstairs, grabbed the key sitting next to the front door, and walked out.

No one had bothered to ensure that he wouldn't leave. Perhaps because they believed he lacked courage, or maybe because they anticipated a manhunt, in which his chances of survival would be slim. Tristan had a feeling that it was the second case.

Either way, he was pretty sure they never thought he would go out for a few hours only before coming back. If he hurried and stayed discreet, they probably wouldn't notice he was gone. The cool night air caressed his face with its encouraging hand. Tristan was glad that Caleb's reaction had pleased Aeron and the others, and they hadn't decided to kill him right away. However, even if they had avoided this learned helplessness thing, he knew it was only a reprieve. Sooner or later, they would get bored and kill him. Tristan had to act before that happened.

He headed for the infirmary, where he had seen the woman enter. Nivitha, that was what the girl Aeron had killed had called her. After what had happened, he doubted she would trust him, but he had to try; there was no one else he could turn to.

The building was easily recognizable thanks to a hand-painted sign above the door. Tristan knocked, and a short East-Asian man with a buzzcut opened. He had obviously been in bed, judging by his sleepy look and pajama bottoms. His red and puffy eyes suggested that he had been crying. Two horizontal scars ran across his bare torso.

"Oh shit, what happened to your eye? Come in, we'll take care of it!"

"No!" Tristan exclaimed, "They'll know! I mean, it's okay. Is Nivitha here?"

The man gave him a puzzled look.

"She doesn't work with us anymore. You're safe here, don't worry. Let me at least disinfect it."

Tristan hesitated but eventually agreed. There was no reason for the gang to find out, and he didn't want to die of sepsis. The man, who said his name was Lucas, made him sit down on a chair and gently took care of the empty eye socket. The pain made Tristan flinch a few times, but when Lucas was done, he had to admit that he felt a little better.

"You really don't want to tell me what happened?" the man asked kindly.

Tristan shook his head. He had a rather ordinary appearance, and people usually didn't pay attention to him. However, if he talked about the group, he was afraid the man would remember seeing him with them. This would reduce his chances of getting information about Nivitha to nothing. To his relief, the man gave him a sympathetic smile and did not insist.

"You're looking for Nivitha, right? What do you want with her?"

"I want to check on her, see how she's holding up," Tristan lied, "I know it's late, but I just heard the news and I'm worried about her."

Lucas smiled sadly at him.

"That's very nice of you. I'm worried too, but she won't talk to us anymore. I hope she'll agree to see you. She shouldn't be alone at a time like this."

He told him how to find the building where she lived. Tristan thanked him warmly and left. He wondered if it was his injury that made Lucas think he was not a threat, or if he was naturally trusting. He could only hope that things would go as smoothly with Nivitha.

Nivitha was awakened by knocks on the door. She pushed back her blanket angrily and stood up. Telling Lucas where she was going had been a mistake. She had thought that would reassure him enough to leave her alone, but obviously she had been mistaken. Ready to tell him exactly what she thought of his inaction, she opened the door, but stopped dead in her tracks when she came face to face with Tristan instead.

He opened his mouth to speak, but Nivitha didn't give him the time. Blinded by hatred and sadness, she grabbed him by his blue scarf and slammed him violently against the wall.

"You killed my sister! She was kind and bright and she's dead because of you!"

She could barely keep from crying.

"I'm sorry," he breathed.

Nivitha was taken aback by the pain in his voice. Only then did she notice that his right eye was gone. She took a step back, unsure, remembering that it was because he had stumbled that she had been able to flee.

"What are you doing here?" she asked coldly, ready to renew his encounter with the wall if his answer didn't please her.

"Caleb needs help," he answered, looking at her imploringly with his only remaining eye.

Nivitha studied him carefully, trying to determine if she could trust him. He reminded her of a wounded rabbit, sad and terrified. Then there was his eye, which couldn't have disappeared by itself.

"What happened?" she asked, pointing to the empty socket.

Tristan winced.

"They got angry that you got away because of me. I don't have much time, listen, please."

Tristan was cowering in on himself, as if afraid she would hit him at any moment. She let him speak, and he explained the general situation to her.

"I thought of slitting their throats in their sleep," he concluded, "but if one of them wakes up and alerts the others, I'm dead. That's why I need help. You don't happen to have a gun, by any chance?"

Nivitha assessed the situation. She had a feeling he was sincere, and besides, he was her best chance to find Caleb rapidly. It was a risk she had to take.

"No, and I don't know where to find any. What about them?"

"No." Tristan shrugged, "Too easy and not personal enough, whatever that means."

Nivitha winced. It was good for them, but this reasoning made her deeply uncomfortable.

"Then we'll cut their throats. We'll start with the most dangerous ones, so even if they wake up the others when they die, we'll still have eliminated the two biggest threats." she suggested.

Tristan nodded.

"The biggest threat is Aeron, but if we're talking about pure strength, it's Isaac and Brenna. I want to save Aeron for last, so he can see my face before he dies."

Despite Tristan's words, Nivitha felt more pain than anger in his voice.

"Okay, but I want him to see me too. He's the one who killed Asha."

"Then we'll kill him together."

This plan was fine with Nivitha. It was far from perfect, but it was at least less of a suicide mission than his original idea. There was one thing that bothered her, though.

"We should start by freeing Cal, in case something goes wrong. Like, if we all kill each other or something..."

"Aeron has the key, I can't get it without killing him."

"Then I'll take a pair of wire cutters. I know where to find some." Nivitha insisted, her tone allowing no contradiction.

"Fine," Tristan conceded, "then you'll wait for me tomorrow night in front of Aeron's house. Parts of the walls have collapsed, but it would be too loud to climb them. I'll come and open the door for you when everyone is asleep, and we'll do what we have to do."

Caleb was partying. Amongst all the blurry faces around him, those of Nivitha and Tristan stood out. They were dancing together to the pop music that the speakers were blaring, and motioned for him to join them. When he did, their faces transformed and twisted into a terrifying mask of anger.

"You abandoned us," they snarled in unison. "You could have helped us, but you only cared about yourself. You are selfish, selfish!"

Other voices echoed:

"Selfish, selfish, you are selfish."

Caleb could see a woman with one of her breasts gouged out, a skinned man, charred figures. He wanted to run, but Aeron, Brenna, Isaac, and Lola blocked his path.

"You deserve everything that has happened to you, you are selfish, selfish!"

Caleb closed his eyes and pressed his hands to his ears in a desperate attempt to silence them.

He woke up with a start, drenched in sweat, and saw Tristan tapping gently on the bars.

"Help is coming," the young man whispered so softly that Caleb barely heard him, "Tomorrow night. Everything will be okay."

As the young man settled on the floor with the towel that he used as a blanket, a timid spark of hope stirred within Caleb. He dared to dream that Tristan was really going to put an end to all this torture. His nightmare came back to his mind and a wave of nausea washed over him. Tristan was taking huge risks to help him, when he himself had never done anything for him. Whatever his plan, it was bound to be dangerous. He debated whether he really deserved his help. He wasn't sure anymore, but he had to get out of here, no matter what. Caleb promised himself that if he made it out alive, he would do everything he could to make up for it.

Caleb fell back into a restless sleep. He was awakened by a grunt of pain. He opened his eyes and saw Aeron kicking Tristan, who was curled up in his towel.

"So, nerd, how's your eye?" the man with the tattooed arm sneered.

"I'm sorry, I told you, it was an accident. I tripped, it won't happen again, I promise!" Tristan moaned.

"Yeah, you better. Don't imagine you're forgiven just because we gouged out your eye, that was just a warning. Now go make us some breakfast."

Tristan stood up with difficulty and complied. Once again, Caleb wondered what he had done. If Aeron had found out he'd given him water, he couldn't have made it look like an accident, so maybe it had to do with the plan.

The day stretched on and on. It was one of those days when Aeron and his gang stayed in the basement, smoking and chilling. Tristan didn't have a moment's rest; when Aeron wasn't asking him to clean the floor or the walls, it was Isaac who wanted a beer, Lola who asked him to rearrange the cupboard, or Brenna who wanted a massage.

Caleb eagerly awaited the night, a mix of anxiety and anticipation swirling within him. Besides enduring the occasional cage-kicking, the only time anyone paid attention to him was when Isaac would take him out for his evening meal.

He drank the cold soup and water with a straw through the muzzle. Despite his hunger, he couldn't stand the taste anymore and longed to eat a real meal again.

Some time later, everyone finally went to bed, including Tristan. Caleb stared at him, waiting for something to happen. An hour passed, without the young man moving. Caleb was getting more and more anxious, when the young man finally stood up. Tristan nodded to him and walked up the stairs that led out of the basement. When he came back down, Caleb thought he was dreaming. Nivitha was there, behind him, a wire cutter in one hand and a kitchen knife in the other. He almost burst into tears when he saw her, but managed to remain silent. Nivitha approached him and skillfully severed the lock that had kept him imprisoned, while Tristan stood guard.

"What have they done to you?" Nivitha murmured in horror, "We'll take care of you as soon as we get rid of them, I promise, but if anything happens, just leave us and run, okay?"

She moved towards Brenna without giving Caleb time to protest. Tristan did the same with Isaac, and Caleb noted that he too was holding a kitchen knife. They exchanged a look, nodded, and simultaneously slit Brenna and Isaac's throats. Their deaths were not instantaneous, as Caleb would have expected. Blood spurted from the gaping wounds, and Brenna and Isaac twitched and groaned weakly for a few moments.

Tristan and Nivitha quickly muffled the noise with pillows, but it had been enough to wake Lola. She slowly approached Tristan, her knife in hand. Tristan could not see her because of his missing eye. Caleb wanted to yell at him to be careful, but that would have woken Aeron up. He gathered his courage and strength and, ignoring the pain that was taking all his limbs hostage, he threw himself at Lola. The young woman spun around, and the blade that should have sunk into Tristan's carotid artery slashed Caleb's arm instead. Lola wasn't a fighter, but she had no trouble overpowering Caleb after all the injuries he'd suffered in the last two weeks. She raised her knife to kill him, and suddenly froze. Her eyes widened in incomprehension as a few drops of blood flowed from her mouth and throat, from which the tip of a blade protruded. The blade was withdrawn and Lola collapsed, revealing Tristan breathing heavily, the bloody knife in his hand.

The two young men did not have time to feel relieved; Aeron had been awakened by the commotion. After a few seconds of shock, had rushed at Nivitha, his switchblade wielding in front of him. Nivitha raised her arms to protect herself, and the blade went through her left hand, sinking a little less than half an inch into the skin under her eye. The young woman pressed her hand until the blade went all the way through, and then grabbed the handle and pulled it away from Aeron. Startled, he did not react quickly enough. Nivitha's kitchen knife was pressed against his throat while he himself was unarmed. Tristan joined her and pressed his own blade against Aeron's abdomen.

"This is for Asha," Nivitha began.

"And for me, and for Caleb, and for all those you hurt," Tristan finished, his voice shaking with rage and pain.

"Wait!" Aeron exclaimed, "I..."

Nivitha and Tristan did not give him time to elaborate. Together, they thrust their blades into his flesh and watched him bleed to death. The relief was overpowering as they witnessed him struggle to breathe through the slit in his throat which produced disgusting gurgling sounds. The red stain was growing rapidly on his white shirt, and it soon merged with the cascading streams from his throat. Aeron quickly lost consciousness, and less than a minute later, he was dead.

Nivitha felt the same satisfaction she had felt with the two men, mixed with a hint of cruel joy. It wouldn't bring her sister back, she knew, but now she was avenged and those bastards would never make another victim.

As soon as she was sure he was really dead, Nivitha rushed towards Caleb. She almost took him in her arms, but held back at the last moment for fear of hurting him. Instead, she ran her hand through his light pink hair.

"It's okay, we'll get you out of here," she said soothingly.

Caleb opened his mouth to speak, but a sob came out instead. Tristan delicately took his hand, and Caleb clung to it as if his life depended on it.

"Don't worry, there is an infirmary, we will take you there, everything will be fine."

Caleb couldn't stop crying. He nodded, and Nivitha helped him up while Tristan wrapped a towel around him to hide his nakedness. Caleb's whole body hurt, and his friends had to half carry him out of the basement. The cool night air made him shiver, but comforted him at the same time. It was really over; he was finally out of hell.

Pet

Epilogue: 3 months later

Caleb woke up snuggled between his two partners. He looked at them with a sad smile. None of them were okay: Nivitha had a small pale tear-shaped scar under her left eye and a bigger one on her hand, where Aeron's knife had pierced it. Tristan's right eye, or rather the place where it had been, was covered with a white cloth patch. As for himself, Caleb was covered in scars from head to toe, a reminder of the screws, the lashes, the burns, and all the torture that Aeron and the others had put him through.

The real scars, the ones that still made them suffer, were not visible. They were carved deep into their souls and would never fully disappear.

Tristan sighed in his sleep and pressed himself a little closer to him. Caleb stroked his brown hair and smiled. They may not have been okay, but the three of them had found a kind of peace together. They understood each other and could rely on one another, and day after day, the pain became a little easier to bear, a little less suffocating.

Tristan and Nivitha had immediately started working in the infirmary. It was an obvious choice for Tristan, who was making the most of what he had learned in medical school. For Nivitha, Caleb had quickly figured out that it was more complicated, and that she had only taken this role to be by his side as much as possible. When he had asked her, she had explained why she had left them after Asha's death.

Lucas had eventually come to apologize, as had most of her coworkers, and as the weeks went by, she had come to feel more or less comfortable among them again. Once Caleb left the infirmary, she alternated between her old job and working in the field with Bernadette and George. Caleb had decided to work in the infirmary as well. He cleaned wounds, handed out food and water, and spent a lot of time making sure the younger patients and those without family or friends felt safe. He didn't want anyone to feel as scared, alone and lost as he had.

That's why, when he learned that some survivors had opened an orphanage, he made it a point to go there regularly to read stories to the children and spend time with them. He even started to teach some of them how to do macramé.

Despite this, Caleb, who had once been so comfortable in a crowd, could not help but be apprehensive around people now. He wanted to help, and he did as much as he could, but sometimes he couldn't stand being out of the apartment. He spent long hours there with Tristan and Nivitha, the only two people he felt completely safe with. Despite Lucas' invitation, the three of them had decided to stay in Nivitha's apartment, far from the crowd, in their own little haven of peace.

Caleb softly kissed Tristan's lips, then Nivitha's, and got up, soon followed by his two partners. It was time to get ready for work, to make this new world as welcoming as possible.

Afterword

Thank you so much for your support! If you enjoyed this book, feel free to leave a review, I'd love to know what you thought of it. If you didn't enjoy it, feel free to leave a review too, but in that case, I might not love to know what you thought about it.

If you want to stay updated on my work, you can follow me on Instagram: @author_aiden.e.messer

Best wishes,
Aiden E. Messer

About the author

Aiden E. Messer does not exist. Are they an illusion, a ghost, a mere thought? No one knows. If we are to believe one of the children they seem to work with, if they were a teacher, they would be as tall as a human. They are not a teacher. According to various sources, they have studied psychology, and have always had a penchant for horror and the macabre. They like to combine his subjects in their books.

About the illustrator

Pastek is a weird lil creature from Switzerland. They write comics about science and perhaps dumb stories too. Sometimes they take a break from drawing cute furries and create some disturbing shit because their twisted lil brain needs a break. In their free time they enjoy being gay and kind but extremely annoying.

Their website: pastek.ch

Printed in Great Britain
by Amazon